In any bar at night
I meet goddess acolytes
With lust beyond their tawny hose;
Stray eyes search me, never meek,
Knowing what I know,
Selling what I seek,
Promising on soft blonde thighs,
Cleverness beyond the wise.

From COMPLINE, Cantos Pantera
by Tony Barnard

Also by Len Vinchi, DOG SOUL,
a Fantasy Horror Novel
Surreal, mystic and violent, DOG SOUL
explores the wolf in man

Man Rape
by Len Vinchi

Madeleine Shaw ♦ Publishers
London

MAN RAPE

by

Len Vinchi

© Len Vinchi 2000

ISBN 1 9007 3727 2

First Edition
First Published in the UK, 2000

Published by
Madeleine Shaw Publishers
PO Box 10024
London E8 1PT

Printed and bound in Great Britain by:
Madeleine Shaw,
PO Box 10024, London E8 1PT

PROLOGUE

ESKALITH, Babylon, 689 BC.

In 689 BC, the great city of Babylon fell to the Assyrians under Sennacherib, their king, who captured Eskalith, beautiful high priestess of the Babylonian Temple. Though he desired her, she would not submit to him. In fury, Sennacherib crucified her, in April, mocking the religion she stood for, that of the recurrent rebirth of the Great Goddess every spring.

Eskalith was taken from the cross by five of her surviving female acolytes. They washed and cleansed her body, perfumed her with incense, frankincense and myrrh, put cloves and aloes on her, strewed her with red rose petals, dressed her in her red silk gown, and buried her with a mirror, so she could see her beauty in the after life. But they forgot that rats can chew through lead caskets.

CHAPTER ONE

For the first time in a generation, a light showed in the first floor of a boarded up women's clothing shop called Nunnery. Sam Reese had at last returned to Charnegate, a bustling area of the East End of London, next to Spitalfields with its famous white-stoned, high-steepled church, Christ Church, and wholesale fruit and vegetable market. It was spring, not that you could tell by the weather that evening, it was misty, and cold winds flew down Commercial Street to the river Thames.

He sat on a stool beneath the skylight, but could see no moon, nor stars, because of the mist, which was like an opaque blanket. Sam sat by his cutting table. He was a tall guy, not quite yet forty, with a mop of ash blonde hair, big pendulous pink lips, very white skin. An unusual face, but handsome. It was 9 pm. Around him was a low dull roar, like a dirty sea breaking upon a refuse-infested shore - the slick of noise made up of traffic, the hum of electricity, the quake of the underground trains, the million conversations in pubs, restaurants, cabs, bars. In the midst of so much light and darkness, at the centre of Babel, Sam sat on his stool sketching, his Senior Service cigarette giving off a thin blue plume.

The gleam of his father's shears winked dully at him as the fluorescent light dimmed as the spark faltered. It was amazing they'd survived, he could still see where the fire had burnished the steel, but it was good Sheffield stainless and would see many a yard of cloth cut under his hands.

He got up. Saw again just how good the room was, twenty feet by twelve, just four walls, a door and a skylight. Large side windows. Bolts of cloth lay in their racks, bought that day from Liberty's. In the corner on an old table was his father's Singer sewing machine, another survivor of the holocaust. Yes, it was going to be great.

He would earn good money, real money. He would make it, doing what he always wanted to do, make beautiful clothes for good-looking girls, to adorn the female architecture.

Without warning, hatred rose in his gullet like bile, until he could scarce swallow the cooling coffee by his hand. Scarce smoke. Scarce breathe.

Then he smiled slowly to himself, was he getting morbid? All those years wasted from 1967 to now, Spring, 1990, were like death on his heart. Well, old son, *you* did it. *You* took four tabs of LSD. You might have died.

He made some more coffee. Count of small mercies, old son, by rights you shouldn't be here. Not here in Charnegate, not here among the living. The living? How did he know the ten thousand he passed by in Commercial Street were living? For all he knew, there were walking undead in the crowds. Frankenstein with a face lift. Dracula in a Savile Row suit and a pint of NHS blood in his veins, maybe. Robots. How could you know otherwise? There was that old saying, You might entertain angels unawares. Well, if angels, why not a demon or two? Who would know unless they told you in some way? How do you tell the mugger in the crowd until he actually mugs you? The walking undead were there, for all he or anyone really knew. Don't look at their faces, you might see something - so no one in big cities ever looked at anyone else. Golden opportunity.

Sam forced a smile. Come on, get on with it.

His powerful hands stitched gold thread into lame with speed and precision. The fluorescent lighting in its periodic flashing was not ideal to work under, and he planned to have pearl bulbs installed instead. His late father Ben, he recalled, swore by fluorescent lighting, and it was an idiosyncrasy of most tailors that they had their own fetish about lighting. Some would only work by daylight, others by various forms of electric lighting. There was one old biddy down Mile End who worked by gas light.

Well, he'd come back, he was cured, nothing was going to stop him now. No one, either, even if he knew that all he had to do was turn round to be confronted by the misted mass of Convent, across bustling Commercial Street, one time nunnery, Convent, where a tall, black-suited man sat smoking a cheroot, in his lighted office, *looking directly into the studio*. Beamish Smiley. Undertaker.

He wouldn't turn round. All that was over. But...

For Chrissakes! Sam cursed himself, it's your illness making you think that guy had anything to do with it. Sam, old son, you took LSD, and now you take medicinal drugs to damp down your imagination, to shut off the shrieking synapses of the schizophrenic, so the skull was not so full of demons. Sedative tranquillisers muted the shrieks, toned down the colours, deodorised the smells, so he could still think. Without his medication he would have been in thrall, helpless against his LSD-induced illness. He had to understand the terror was in *him* - not out there.

He pictured long-legged, full-busted girls, hair shining, lips wet and luscious. Girls he would dress. He smiled, it was going to be great.

The light still shone in the studio at midnight, and one also shone in Convent across the street.

CHAPTER TWO

When Sam's psychiatrist, Dr Jacob Harowitz, was promoted to Consultant of Hanwell Mental Hospital in West London, he had Sam transferred there too, from Becknell, the East End catchment mental hospital where Sam had first been committed. Sam's neighbour, Beamish Smiley, had taken him to the casualty department of the London Hospital in his hearse.

Dr Jacob Harowitz was medium height and build, aquiline face and earnest manner. He believed the brain to be pure mechanism. It could go wrong just as a computer could; Sam had fused his brain with LSD - blown the circuitry so he saw everything unfiltered, powerless to control his emotions, swayed this way and that by sudden fears which led him to violent outbursts. Accordingly, Jacob kept him heavily sedated, a zombie state, scarce alive. But what was the way out of this cruel dilemma? Unsedated, Sam was a victim to terrible hallucinations (a woman raping him) and delusions: - all women, were out to hurt him, nurses were going to cut him up. His hallucinations and delusions, Dr Harowitz believed, goaded Sam to fury, left him shaking, wet with sweat. And suicidal. *Sedated*, he was just sat and stared, or drew horrible pictures of himself being groped. Dr Harowitz tried to do the best he could, and given the state of medical knowledge, that meant, for most of the time, all he could do was spare his patient emotional pain.

And this had included trying to prevent visits by Beamish Smiley. His visits reduced Sam to frothing at the mouth with anger, even when almost comatose on Largactile. Jacob was puzzled, but had no option but to tell Smiley in no uncertain terms that his visits would not be permitted. For all that, it was many months before Smiley ceased to appear in Jacob's office inquiring for news. But there was never any to give him.

The first decade of hospitalisation had seen Sam mostly in a locked ward, where patients are not allowed out except under supervision.

Hanwell was built for thousands of Victorian mentally ill. It was huge, a city of its own, with kitchens, workshops, lawns, churches, and wards. Some wards consisted of tiny cubicles with iron bars at the window. In these were enclosed the violent and the unrestrainable, with straitjackets, shackles, bands and belts. By 1981 when Sam got there, drugs were used more often and were more effective, though jackets and soft cells were still a part of the regime.

But Sam was no longer violent enough to be in a locked cell or even a locked ward. He could walk the grounds of this huge hospital, take cups of tea in the canteen, go to the various workshops, play soccer in the winter, cricket in the summer. Sometimes a nurse would take him walking along Brunel's canal, where huge locks once lifted the thousands of longboats which travelled Birmingham, Manchester, Limehouse Cut, Port of London. It was a semi-rural area, with fresh air, and he could see rabbits in the fields, even though it was but twenty minutes drive to Central London - if the traffic was not too congested.

For many years there was little change in Sam, and Jacob nearly despaired. His young patient still insisted that something had happened *before* he took the LSD, something in Convent, where terrible things were done to him by... a woman. He insisted he'd taken the LSD *because* of what happened, to get away from the memory. But Jacob said what he described just couldn't happen, there was no woman alive who had the strength or anatomical features which could draw blood, let alone do the other things Sam said she did to him. It was merely hallucination, and that until Sam realised that, he could make no progress.

His wounds were indeed terrible, scar tissue in mouth and between his legs now, but schizophrenics *did* mutilate themselves. Far better that Sam understood that, then he could really begin to heal.

'You lost your mother, and before that your father, both in tragic circumstances. Then you went back to your home in Charnegate, unsettled, after you left boarding school. All in all, it's not surprising you became ill, you took a very very heavy dose of acid. Makes me sick to think you got it at the going away party at your school, bought the tabs for a dare, didn't you?'

How many times had Jacob been through that? On each repetition, and under the influence of drugs, Sam began to doubt that he'd taken the acid to escape from memories of what happened to him. Yes, yes, he tried to convince himself under Jacob's prompting that the LSD brought that hallucination on.

As time went by, Sam's drawings changed, and when Jacob saw the lovely figures of beautiful women that came from Sam's pencil, inks and charcoal, he was entranced. Here was proof positive, the doctor felt, that his treatments really worked. Not only had Sam freed himself from drawing nightmares, he had gradually weaned himself from fears of women.

For him it was only that women in Convent who had to be feared - though he now went along with Jacob and said she was a hallucination.

Jacob for his part, like many a forward looking physician in the old hospitals, was more than happy for Sam to strike up friendships with young women patients. It was all part of the real healing process.

No matter how hypersensitive Sam might be, he no longer suffered from the most crippling aspects of schizophrenia. He could relate the hours of the day with his life, could plan, could think a problem through. Often his imagery would be bizarre, but no one really knew how awful other people's mind- sets were. If they could turn up for work and hold a banal conversation, they didn't need much more to function in a big city like London. Furthermore, his illness, or rather the scars of that illness, made him sensitive to nuances which other people undoubtedly missed. When he drew his fingers over silk, it felt like sandpaper, while real sandpaper was like shards of glass, or upturned fragments of razor blades. He could tell denier of a stocking by merely placing his finger on it, preferably when a girl had her leg in it. He could detect sounds better too, no one could fool him they liked him merely by smiling, for he listened to the intonation of the voice and could easily detect the harshness that spoke of repugnance, or the stridency that revealed irritation. Smells were so powerful, it was like having them stuck up his nose on meat skewers, thrust into the nasal membranes and twisted to set off the response. He could tell when a girl had been with a man, when she was menstruating, all this no matter how many showers she had, or what deodorant she used. It was useful, because he could tell when she was relaxed, and he learned how to find the right words to relax his lovers.

Jacob and Sam could often be seen walking the grounds together, and it would be difficult to tell who was the physician, who the patient, for on a high summer's afternoon all you would see would be two men in their thirties, wearing jeans and shirts, long-haired, in close conversation. Friends.

In the summer of 1986, as they strolled along the canal bank, Sam was saying to Jacob, 'Can I have the tools for dressmaking?'
Jacob looked into his face, saw the calmness there, the desire to make clothes balanced by the knowledge that Jacob could deny him. 'What do you need?'
Jacob did not really know what was involved. Sam told him about a flat table, cloth, and shears. Jacob ruminated, shears sounded dangerous, but then what could be more

dangerous than a chisel or a hammer, yet patients were allowed to use these in certain circumstances in the workshops, so there was no *a priori* grounds for rejection. He decided to give Sam his head.

Sam's dresses were soon famous, he was so skilful a designer, so brilliant a cutter, and even sewer, that his wonderful garments attracted the admiration of nurses and doctors, and this filtered to the wives of consultants and administrators. They brought, under Sam's supervision, fine silks, velvets, brocades, satins, and he would measure them, and show them sketches of designs, or translate their vague ideas into sketches which they loved.

He did all this work in the corner of the occupational therapy (soft toys) room. Patients around him would be making stuffed teddy bears, or cushions.

His father, Ben Reese, a tailor himself, had always said Sam would never make a tailor, he was too artistic. He was a dressmaker - far better in Sam's opinion to kneel in front of a girl, or even an old woman, than rub against the crotch of some supercilious sod, which he'd seen his father do so many times. Which way do you dress, sir? You didn't have to ask that of a woman, and they smelled better. And besides, sometimes they were beautiful, and then it was pure pleasure measuring them.

One afternoon, when Sam and Jacob were having a cup of tea and a cigarette together, Sam realised that in all the years he had know Jacob, he had never seen him laugh. Oh Jacob, he thought, you've carried so much for me.

In that moment, Sam knew he was stronger, better, that he had no place in the Hospital any more. He asked Jacob to discharge him. Jacob smiled.

All the myriad of services involved agreed, Sam could function out there in what was euphemistically called the community. They had no doubt about Sam, he could cope.

Technically, he would now be given the status of voluntary patient, which meant he could discharge himself.

He did so twenty-three years after being committed. He was in good spirits at the farewell party which he hosted and financed, in the staff common room of his section of wards. But beneath his calm, hope and hatred railed one against the other.

At the end of the afternoon hour's festivities, he shook hands with Jacob and left in a taxi - for Charnegate, his flat, his studio.

CHAPTER THREE

A few days after he had come back, Sam was making himself a cup of instant coffee and worrying about his health visitor, Miss Mae Fields, whom he had never met and who was due in a few minutes' time. Bet she'll be one of those condescending little tarts who treat you as an equal. He smiled and lit another cigarette, looking out of the window at Convent. It loomed grey in the slight fog of late morning, London. Just what would a National Health worker make of that? he wondered, that bloody mausoleum where so much of his life lay secret, his mother, his father, and himself, the place of his rape - alleged rape, really, nothing more than a delusion, so they'd said.

This knicker-twisted health visitor, this Mae Fields, would have read his case notes, and she'd come with the mind set in a prearranged pattern. Nothing infuriated him more than the wall of zero communication these health professionals put up.

A sudden dash of colour caught his attention across the street, a red-haired girl in jeans and leather jacket, waiting to cross. Now there was a little beauty, no doubt about it. Sharp as a ferret, her, look at the way she sizes it all up. Wonder where she lives? Can see the glint of her green eyes from here, not a big person, but stacked, sharp features, pert nose and a big mouth. He watched her check the time on her wrist, then she came across the road and out of sight.

He smiled to himself and drew on his cigarette, itching to get on with his work but the appointment with his health visitor continued to irritate him. Health visitor - funny name, they were actually sick visitors, wouldn't visit the healthy now, would they?

His concentration momentarily broken, he forgot the girl and wished again the visit was over. He wanted to leave all that behind, get on with life and love, with his skill, his dreams. And then the door bell rang.

He bounded downstairs, opened up, and there was the girl he'd seen.

She smiled and said, 'Hello, Mr Reese, I'm Mae Fields, I'm your health worker.'

The undertaker across the road in his second story office set in Convent, Beamish Smiley, saw Mae go into Sam's. Nice little arse. Probably a social worker judging by he way the two of them are chatting by the window. She's handing him pills. Bloody nuisance, social workers. This one could sod things up, calling on him regularly. She probably knows all about his history, and that means she knows about me. Trust the bloody government to fuck things up when we just had it going nice. Bleeding liberty, calling on people. Invasion of privacy. Still, if she got in the way, there was always a solution to that.

Beamish turned away from his window and poured himself a Scotch. Redheads were always welcome, he smirked, why his own mother had a mop of ginger hair.

Sam found he liked the little visitor in spite of himself. For a start, she called him Mr Reese, instead of presuming to belittle him with use of his christian name as most of them did.

On seeing him, Mae's heart had lurched, he was so tall, so sensitive, and those grey-blue eyes of his were so full of loving, loving that had to come out somewhere.

Sam was transfixed by her, her nearness, her so evident goodness. Who said no one ever loved except at first sight? So you do what men have always done, never a faint heart him, and this was his fair lady, cockney sparrow, bright as a new pin. 'I'll make a dress for you.' He stumbled in his speech. 'I mean, let's go to the flicks. Or would you like to share a bottle of wine with me? I mean, I'll knock up a risotto. Pretty good at that.' He stopped abruptly, seeing she was eyeing him quizzically, smiling a little.

'Tell you what, give me a call.' She wrote out her telephone number on a pad from her handbag and handed him the torn off sheet. 'It'll be a change to talk about nice things, like fashion, I can tell you.'

He nodded, blushing a little, and saw her out. After as he made another coffee, he whistled, he was getting better by the minute. His first date out of hospital, and with a girl who already knew so much about him, and didn't seem to mind.

On her way towards Aldgate East tube, Mae saw a black Rolls Royce hearse come out of Convent. She gasped as she saw the driver, who was leering at her. He seemed the spitting image of Sam Reese, older, and less kind. Why was the geezer clocking her? she wondered, and as she forced herself to ignore him, as images of Sam's past life swirled into her mind. Convent, where he used to say terrible things happened to him, the mysterious death of his mother, and before that his father, Ben Reese, the tailor.

She glanced again at the hearse, now very slowly pulling ahead of her, with Smiley smirking as if he had some private joke which somehow involved her, fixing her with pale grey eyes, eyes the same as Sam's, but hating, not loving. She shuddered. He slowed down at the kerb.

'Want a lift, luv?'

'Sod off, you kerb-crawling creep.'

Smiley laughed dryly, and sped away.

Mae dismissed him from her mind, but the more she got rid of him, the more Same came to her. Christ, she thought, the best thing he could do was get out of Charnegate, start over. The place was too full of memories, too many loose ends.

As the weeks passed by, Beamish Smiley got more and more obsessed with Mae. She was coming regularly to see Sam, and they had a grand old time he guessed. 'Spect the little tart will move in with him. Wasn't that the way things went? Now it was almost certain they'd have to involve her. She was in any case attractive, especially with her pony tail that swished burnished copper in the sun.

'It was just as the docs thought,' Sam said, sitting opposite Mae at the kitchen table which bore the remains of a fish and chip dinner and two steaming mugs of strong tea, 'all an LSD-induced delusion.'

Mae sipped her tea, feeling glad he was optimistic, but not so sure now it was a delusion. Something *had* happened, something *was* happening. Who was this woman in the stories he'd recounted to her over the last few weeks? She came and went like a phantom in his trying to understand the past. And there was another recurring theme, that of mannequins. His father had had two of them, apparently made by Smiley in his side-line shop window, ladies wear, what had happened to them? Sam said he thought he saw them sometimes, in dreams, walking in the streets, but he laughed it off.

'Anyway we're leaving here, starting afresh. I'll get a good price for the old homestead.'

'Those photographs - of your parents, I mean...'

She was testing him out, he realised that, and was ready. 'You mean - have I got over the fact I'm six-two and fair, while my father, Ben, was short and dark? You mean - have I got over the fact that that old sod across the road in Convent probably seduced my mother, and he's my father?'

'I just want to be sure, Sam, that you aren't still obsessed.' She bit her lip, it was the wrong word, it was she who had taken on that state of mind. Sam was ready to throw it away from him, while she was getting more and more curious, horrified, scared but fascinated by the legends and folklore of this area of the East End. How the convent had been closed because the nuns there had been involved in a scandal, illegitimate babies, black masses, suicides and lunacies, until it had been closed down and used as an orphanage, and later Beamish Smiley's mother had inherited it from her father and used it as premises for their undertaking business.

Mae looked out through the window, saw that Convent formed the east border of Charnegate, at the V of two narrow roads, Sepulchre Street and Cripple Way facing Spitalfields, and in the shadow of Christ Church's spire. At the back of Convent was a disused graveyard, and then a red bricked wall, behind which was Mode Place.

Convent presented a gabled front of limestone with a central door, double width of black painted oak, approached through tall wrought iron gates, which had been part of the original convent. There were shrubs of privet bordering the pathway leading to the door. On either side of the gates were iron railings.

It was an imposing, but simple building. Basically it was a largish gabled roof structure, ground floor with two windows at front, tall eight foot windows, one each side of the door, then a row above of three, and then in the gable itself one. Access to these floors was made by the spiral staircase set in the tower which stood a story higher and was adjoined to Convent on the Christ Church side. The window at the gable was arched, and it was here that a figure was standing, that of a red-haired woman. Sam saw her too, and then she was gone.

'The more we dig into it, the worse it gets,' Sam said. 'Let's go, let's forget it all.'

Mae saw the rising colour of hope in his face, how his whole body seemed to yearn to be free of the nightmare years, and she could not deny him that. After all, it was just curiosity on her part. He deserved the chance and, she thought ruefully, so did she. Love didn't always come to people, neither did the possibility of a good future. She would be out of her tree not to go with him, and if she didn't, what on earth would she be thinking of?

'OK, my luv, it's all behind you.'

They clinked tea mugs.

She still had some business to do in her little bedsit, make sure all the bills were paid, and see about leave of absence from her job, and she'd help him shut up shop and pack, and then they'd leave for a holiday, putting the house up for sale, hoping to return to a new life.

Neither of them heard Susannah, a tall, red-haired woman, retreat down the stairs. Minutes later she was with Smiley.

'Artful little trollop, that Mae Fields,' Susannah sneered, 'got him right round her little finger. Not only moved in with 'im, but you'd think they was Darby and Joan.'

'Should've thought what happened to him would have put him off the fairer sex,' joked Smiley, but Susannah was not amused.

'You take care of your gob. Besides they're planning to do a runner, a bleeding holiday.'

'So the birds will fly?' Smiley grimaced.

'Bella will get Sam, but Mae will be more difficult.' Susannah replied, sipping her gin and orange. 'We could pick them up now, I suppose, but-'

'Exactly. We still don't know the details.'

Susannah gave her screeching laugh, 'Don't we?' Then seeing him take her meaning, she continued more matter-of-factly, 'Just you make sure you think of something to make certain they don't fly the coop. Slow 'em down a bit.'

CHAPTER FOUR

Sam lay in bed listening to Mae's snores, they were sibilant rather than rasping, they comforted him. He was also listening to the late night traffic scud Commercial Street, it never really ended, what with the City, and industry North and South. The third of the trio of sounds was the dialogue and terrible background music of the video, a tacky production of *Tomb of Lygia*. Christ, that guy Poe had a mind like a freak show. The beautiful dead woman on the screen slowly came alive as some reveller blared his horn in the street. Bored, he thumbed the remote, and the TV screen died in a wraith of colour.

He bent down and kissed Mae's head, just at the top of the ear. She murmured, continued to snore, but he could feel her telling him to go to sleep. Maybe he should take some more pills, but he was so happy to have her with him, he wanted to enjoy it all. He got up, shuffled to the kitchen, and made himself some black Nescafe, then went to his cutting table. He opened a drawer and took out a pile of sketchbooks. Shuffled them till he found a red one with a white self-adhesive label on the cover, which was neatly labelled in biro, Way out Designs.

He stirred the sugar goo at the bottom of the black treacly coffee, lit a cigarette, and read his notes. Then he had another idea to make his way of life even more unhealthy. He already had the coffee (doctors tell you it is addictive, gives heart attacks); sugar (other doctors tell you it makes obesity); and tobacco (lung cancer, of course) - but it might be their telling you all this that caused anxiety which brought about the malady, a self-perpetuating death machine in the name of health, was modern medicine, you would not get him near a hospital again. And the idea was *alcohol* (brain degeneration, lipid liver, DTs). He ambled up, fag drooping from his lower lip and got a bottle of Bells, laced his caffeine treacle with a good belt. Great. He now had four of the perfidies in the modern lexicon of sin.

He flipped through the rest of the notebook, dozens of ideas for dresses, frocks, swimsuits, lingerie. Fantastic. After several good belts of Scotch, he went to bed.

So exuberant was Sam with having found Mae, he awoke, not with the blinding hangover his previous night's drinking should greet him with, nor with the furred tongue of the hot coffee drinking smoker, nor indeed with an impaired appetite that sugar should bequeath when taken in such large amounts, but with a healthy desire for a big breakfast, a body taut with energy, a mouth feeling fresh and wholesome, and a mind that was crystal clear.

Mae called from the kitchen, 'Get your shower, then come and get it, big boy.'

He could smell bacon, hear it sizzling, smelled ground coffee, so he reached for a cigarette, and forgot to take it out of his mouth when eventually he ambled into the shower cubicle. He stood there letting the warmth and the water do their work, which they did so well. After, he sat down at the breakfast table, he took in the eggs, took in the bacon, the fried bread, the sliced tomatoes, well juiced in cooking oil, the single fat pork sausage, the Heinz tomato ketchup bottle, and felt almost at peace with the world, his belly cooing to be fed. He began to eat, listening with half an ear to Capitol's mix of absurdly truncated news reports, bad ads and splattered music, another half listened to Mae talking to herself about dinner that evening. He called it talking to herself, because although she was addressing her remarks to him, he never countered any of her suggestions. It was a law of life he had been astute enough to learn at the beginning of their relationship: never argue with the cook. Besides, she had enough counter suggestions of her own, with her, 'Early asparagus? Good, this time of year. I'll drop by in Spitalfields, chat up a wholesaler, tell him there's lots I'm going to buy, be a good customer. Mind you, I wouldn't be seen dead getting greens in Marks & Spencer. Diabolical I call it. You should see the prices they put on their stuff. Myself, I think they have gone over the top. Kind of fascist retailers, and they are always in the right. 'We haf ways of making you buy.' Not that the food is very good anyway, not in my book. You compare the meat you pay through the nose for there with what you get from a good butchers. If you know where to go, you can do well. Yes, I think a roast of Irish beef. Get that from Spencers. Not bloody likely!' And on she went, weaving herself deeper into his heart as she did so.

Sam demolished three eggs, three rashers of bacon, two tomatoes, one large piece of fried bread, half a bottle of ketchup and the large fat sausage, and was now eating brown bread, Hovis, slices with butter and marmalade. There were few things on earth as good as butter melting into toast beneath a layer of Robinsons marmalade. What happened to the little golliwog on the label? He used to collect the labels when he was a kid and send them in, you got a nice enamel golliwog brooch. Wonder if they still make them? But he was also looking at Mae, in her tight Levis, high heeled black shoes, snug white T-shirt and Italian leather black bomber, she looked about seventeen. She had her red hair in a ponytail this morning, and there was no make up on her face, it was a fetish of hers not to use cosmetics often.

'Well, I'm off,' she said, and left for work as he blew her a kiss.

He was still wearing his National Health pyjamas and dressing gown. He got up carrying his mug of coffee, this one had Goofy on, and went to the bedroom. He pulled his clothes on, worn blue jeans, a white T-shirt, with Noddy on, and a pair of ancient trainers, no socks. He then went out to try and get a commission for one of his designs from a local dress manufacturer, and he had high hopes, Spitalfields was full of them, Jewish, English, and Punjabi.

Two hours later, Sam dejectedly climbed the stairs to his flat. He'd been turned down.

Oh, well not to worry old son, it's just that you'll never earn a real crust until someone takes up your designs and makes them in thousands, because after all, you're really doing just couture work, and that never paid, was just a shop window for the bread and jam.

Look on the bright side, you have Mae - and that was the rub, he wanted to give her everything.

The contents of three packets of frankfurters were boiling in a saucepan, the Belling toasted bread. Just a gulp of Scotch (it was half a tumbler, down the hatch in one go). Meal on plate. Lashings of Coleman's mustard. He got each frankfurter down between toast and another slug of Scotch.

When he was finished, burped, and lit a Senior Service.

Fondly, he thought of Mae again, and what she'd done before taking up care work with the mentally ill -running round TV studios, doing up faces of the stars, carrying her little bag of unguents, powders, blushers, false hair, lipsticks, mascaras, eye-liners, gels, aerosols, cotton buds, real sponges, cleansers, moisturisers, brushes and orange sticks, entering the studios of Channel Four in Charlotte Street, TV-AM in Camden Town, her old haunt, Shepherds Bush, as well as independent video-makers, of which there were many in media city, London, transforming ordinary faces into works of art. One day at Shepherds Bush, next Pebble Mill, Birmingham, no wonder threw it in, not that she sat on her little but now.

If before there was every reason to really try and make a go of it, to put the years of hospital behind him, now there was an even greater incentive. He wasn't in by himself any more.

The telephone rang. Minutes later, Sam was on his way down Commercial Street to see the solicitor who had phoned him that afternoon, right out of the blue.

CHAPTER FIVE

While at her bedsit, Mae made her routine phone call to Jacob to report on Sam's progress.

'Yes, he's fine. You'd hardly guess.'

'Well,' replied Sam's doctor, 'I'm pleased to hear that. I must admit I had some doubts about him going back to his old haunts, but I wanted to give him all the support I could. He should be OK if you keep him up with his medication.'

'Funny thing, though,' Mae said, 'he doesn't remember me.'

'I'm not surprised, Mae, after all, when you were doing your training here, he was on a very heavy regime of therapy, and though it was only three years ago, he still had relapses. Anyway, you enjoy your holiday. Going away with anyone I know?' he laughed.

Yes I am, thought Mae, but I won't tell you, and probably if things go well I'll be resigning now I've got Sam. 'Just a little relaxation.'

'OK, I'll look forward to hearing from you, and Sam will be fine for a week or so.'

Then she got on with packing her things from her bedsit, and as she did so, she realised that there was no one to say goodbye to. That was another bond between her and Sam, both had lost their parents, although in her case they both had gone the same time, in an aircrash, a package tour that ended at the Pearly Gates. Oh well, nothing gained by mopsing.

It wasn't actually a secret Mae had about Sam, only that they'd been lovers when she was in training at Hanwell. That had been kept secret at the time, or course, but now her heart went out to him, her lover in the past, who now so clearly lover her again, and yet did not remember her! Now he must be confused to feel such passion and think it came from the present, this moment, when they had spent so many hours together, hours that would have gone into a lifetime if he hadn't insisted they should break off, because, he said it was not fair to her all the time he was a patient, a patient committed under the Mental Health Act, not free to leave until he was adjudged well.

There had been many lonely tears she shed, but in the end she had seen she might impede his progress and there was after all the added risk they would be found out, and what could that do to him? And her? It was not merely a matter of a career, it was Sam she cared about.

And so she went elsewhere to work, and that was helpful, even if it felt cruel. Then he appeared to really forget her, as he did now. Forget her, yet love her! As for her, she had always loved him, and now, by the mere flick of a manager's pen on a timetable for allocation to recently discharged patients, she was here again with him. Not once had she balked at seeing him again, and she was glad, even if it was so bittersweet.

It was sweet to love him, but it was also bitter, for she knew about his body the way a woman can a man's, and though his medical records contained descriptions of his wounds, wounds his doctors insisted were self-inflicted as was possible in schizophrenics, she had always wondered: could it have been true that he had been raped, by a woman, and so viciously? Well, even he had left that behind, apparently believing his illness caused him to hurt himself. If he had been discharged from hospital partly on the assumption that taking Jacob's explanation on board was a proof of his sanity, shouldn't she let sleeping dogs lie? After all, there was time enough for them - she was young and he was hale, what could they not achieve together with a love that was strong and unique in its origins, and now its rebirth, its flowering forth?

Mae knew one thing, she would help, protect, and love him.

Dear, dear Sam, my lovely dressmaker.

When Mae got back to Sam's at six, she found on the kitchen table several bottles of Courage beer, a bottle of white plonk, and three large crabs from a fish stall in Whitechapel. Sat at the table was Sam, smoking, with a big smile on his big face.

'What's this, then, Sam? You come up on the Pools?'

She received no answer, except the popping of a cork, as Sam opened the bottle of plonk. 'Naw, but I may have a dress manufacturer for my designs.'

'Oh Sam, I'm ever so glad for you. Tell me about it.'

'I got this phone call, old guy, my dad's solicitor, Jack Regent...'

Jack Regent, seventy years old, and looking eighty-three, small and wizened like George Burns, had gazed from across the wintry expanse of his teak desk, drew his hands together, made and inverted V with them, and put the tip under his nose. His bifocals glinted, but not so frostily as his brown eyes. He said, 'I had a call from a fellow in the rag trade, says he's seen or heard about your work, and wanted to work something out. Wants you to collect up your best designs, and he'll arrange a time to come and see them.'

Sam was chuffed, but a little less so when he could get no more out of the geezer.

There was no more to be said, except, 'OK, I'll wait for his or your call.'

Jack had said something like, Don't hold your breath, but he couldn't be sure, and he went out of the office.

Still it was worth a celebration, wasn't it, and Mae seemed pleased.

At least they were having a slap up meal.

Wonder who had called? Well, you never knew your luck, guess they could wait a few days before they left.

'Well,' Mae offered, 'just don't build too much hope on it. these days geezers will run you round something cruel. It's the new in thing, to act like an entrepreneur.' She laughed, held up her glass, 'Here's to you kid!'

They touched glasses and drank, then set to the meal, Mae thinking that whatever they had to face together it would be worth it, and for her part, nothing would be too much trouble.

As for Sam, he felt he was really making progress. He was doing work he loved, or at least hoped to, and he had a new girlfriend. True, he had had friends in hospital, but that hardly counted, now he was in the free world. True too there were catches, that sod Smiley offering him so much. Guilt, was it? Or something worse? If only he could recall those years ago when so much happened. It was odd to be told about deaths in the family and not be able to relate to times and dates, even if the grief, the sense of loss, were there.

Ah well, got to get on with it. Love at first sight. Mae! And more Mae, that was the future.

CHAPTER SIX

High up in his office over Commercial Street, Jack Regent was sipping the coffee his secretary had brought him. What was Beamish Smiley playing at? He had a letter of power of attorney drawn up and signed in favour of Sam, a young woman named Mae Fields, individually and jointly (who she?). Decisions affecting his whole life, made in a matter of days. What could be behind it? Then there was the reappearance of Sam. Maybe he should go over and talk with him again, warn him about this so- called dress manufacturer was none other than Smiley. But then, hadn't he accepted Smiley's money, large fees, for a very long time now? Wasn't it a bit late in the day to change the oh so discrete habits of a lifetime? He was, after all, Smiley's lawyer. (But wasn't he also Sam's lawyer, too? His conscience nagged him.) He brushed the idea of going outside his remit firmly aside.

Of course there was something going on, there always had been with Smiley. There was the fact that he let Ben Reese have the shop - Nunnery - for a pittance. The fact that Josie went to work for him in Convent and how she'd been so worried she sent Sam off to boarding school. Just look at the way Ben died, and Josie. But he had in the past been scrupulous: never looked further than he had to to carry out his client's instructions. If he went turning over stones, God knows what might wriggle out. And where would that get him? Once you began poking about, there might be no end to it. He had nothing but a series of strange connexions and he had them only because he was a solicitor. He had no right to try and make sense of the relationships between his clients. Besides, his father had always taught him never to work without a fee. No, he admonished himself firmly, leave well alone.

But it wouldn't quite go away. What stuck in his throat most was what had happened to Sam. There was a young life blighted, if ever there was one. It was an unsettling business, seeing him back after all this time, and that damn shop waiting for him all these years. But he seemed chirpy enough, considering the time he'd spent in hospital. Jack shuddered, he'd already spent too much time cogitating on what did not really concern him.

He got his bowler hat, unaware that he was one of the few men who still wore one, and leisurely made his was out of the office. He was having lunch at Blooms, early, with a client who was getting divorced. Something simple and humdrum, he told himself, unlike this infernal Smiley business.

He liked divorce cases, some of them had been pretty nasty, but even the uncomplicated ones confirmed him in his belief he was right never to have married. Nothing, he believed, could be worth the pain and financial loss a divorce always brought, and strangely it was always the man who seemed to suffer most. He'd read somewhere, probably in the *Sunday Times*, that men faced with living alone for the first time in years often had nervous breakdowns. They couldn't even boil an egg, so they set up with the first complaisant woman who came along. He prided himself on being a good housekeeper, more accurately, flat keeper. He lived in a mews off Brick Lane, two bedroomed. He got his breakfast from cafes on working days, but cooked his own on Sundays. As for laundry, well he had a woman collect it and deliver it, and the intervening mysteries were of no interest to him. Nor was he particularly lonely, there were so many women at the end of a telephone. He only indulged once a month, believing that to do so more often would reduce his natural essences, with a lowering of energy.

All in all, the little man in the bowler hat, the Ben Reese suit, the Crombie overcoat and holding his rolled umbrella, as he threaded his way through the thronged Whitechapel streets, was happy with his lot.

He had forgotten about Beamish by the time he reached Blooms but unfortunately for him, Beamish had not forgotten him.

Beamish had a lot on his mind. At times he felt it was getting out of hand, there was so much to think about and get ready. For one thing, there was the dinner party on April 13th, Good Friday. He knew Susannah was an excellent cook, but it was he who had to work out the menu, and buy the provisions. There were four of them down there, but it was all up to him. He had a crate of a dozen bottles of Margaux, which he found excellent, so the wine was seen to. He doodled with his pencil at his desk on a piece of Conqueror stationery, A-4, with his business address on it. The pencil was a promo item, given to him by his coffin maker, and it said in silver letters along the side, 'Rest Assured our Coffins are Best'. What about a side of beef? Susannah could roast that with potatoes, and asparagus which was plentiful at the moment at Spitalfields. Yes, the idea seemed attractive, he could go down to Smithfields that afternoon and pick up a joint - not frozen - a piece of well-hung Scottish or Hereford beef. Then he'd bring it back and salt it up, he found that improved the taste. All right, he had his main course. Starters? Tomato soup. Fresh. Tomatoes too were plentiful at the moment. And dessert? A fruit salad. Then Lyons Original Blend coffee in a jug, with Cointreau and/or green Chartreuse. He thought he would kick the evening off with Scotch and some wine. He'd been drinking both for years. Decades.

He brightened after finishing these plans - Susannah would approve - felt like a coffee, so swiftly walked to his kitchen, which was as large and as well accoutred.

As he waited for the kettle to boil, he wondered about Sam. This time they wouldn't let him go, that had been the mistake so long past. No mistakes this time.

And that made Smiley think of Jack Regent. Deep in concentration, he poured his coffee, added his Carnation cream, stirred in raw Jamaican brown sugar. Jack would have to dissolve like the sugar, disappear just as the coffee slipped down his throat. Little fart had next to no life force left, he laughed.

Smiley did not trust him, he knew that Jack was very professional, and unless there was money in it for him, he would not even break wind, but Jack was an old man, and he looked it, whereas he, Smiley, was an ancient, and did not look it. That would be enough to make the little turd flip out of sheer envy. It was this that made Beamish certain that sooner or later, Jack would snout around with that bulbous nose of his (what did the shit drink? Sherry? That would be par for the course for him, getting pissed on sherry) and come up with something he could act on, either blackmail or get the Filth in. For years the cops had been receiving complaints about Convent and its owner, and not once had they found anything to pin on him. He knew the police mentality, they had long memories, officers came and went, but the file remained. One day an eager young CID would look at the file and muse, no smoke without fire, and if that officer was fed something strong by Jack, why then there would be trouble. Real trouble. Especially now Sam was here, and him with that cute little slag of his.

Beamish was daydreaming libidinously of what he would like to do to young Miss Mae, and checked himself, there would be time enough for that. Keep it all in the family.

Beamish finished the coffee, flexed his arms, and was just about to head for Smithfield for the beef, when he felt the familiar scratching behind his eyes, gentle this time, like the sharpened claws of very small mice tentatively trying out the surface of the back of his eyes. One of them would be up in a moment. He heard the lift, and a few minutes later Susannah came into the kitchen.

She had her hair done up Grecian style, affixed with a gold chain. He bought that for her about a year ago, cost him five hundred nicker. She didn't have much make-up on today, just some lip gloss, nor was she wearing much, tight jeans and a blouse.

'You worry too much, Beamish. You disturbed us with your worry. I'll see to Jack Regent, don't give it another thought.'

She came up to him and hugged him, charging him with energy, willing life force into him. He felt his bones warm, blood thicken yet flow more easily, felt his muscles increase their tone - all this in a general sense of health and well being. And as usual, his manhood thickened. Susannah laughed, 'My son, the cocksman.' Beamish blushed. Don't you worry, cock, we'll be bringing you something tasty soon.'

She left him feeling good, Who loves his mother? and he felt confident she'd see to the old fart Jack Regent. He only hoped she wouldn't get too excited now the celebration was coming up. When she got high there was no telling what she'd do.

Smiley sucked at his perfect teeth.

Susannah often went out for a bit of rough trade, and always there was some geezer let wondering what had happened to him as he developed diseases that no medical science could cope with. Well, as long as she didn't do it too often, kept it discrete, it wouldn't matter. Who cared about scum like them anyway, picking up young women off the streets?

Certainly not him, he didn't have much to do with low life, him being a Free Mason, and a member of the Chamber of Commerce, respectable businessman him; and besides all that there was that wizened old slag in the preparation room, bloody family wanted the old tart embalmed. Christ, she'd looked like a mummy already. Still with his skills, he'd have her looking like a Barbie Doll for the relatives to gawp at.

And there was the party coming up, and there were two guests, the only two, and these two hadn't even received an invitation. Well, they wouldn't exactly get an invitation! He laughed at his own wit, and went down to the preparation room to embalm the old woman. Just for a bit of fun, he would pull out her brain through her nostrils. Nobody would be any the wiser. Ignorant sods, didn't they know that was how they did it in Egypt? Ask Susannah, she knew a lot.

CHAPTER SEVEN

On his way back from Bloom's, Jack Regent saw Beamish driving his black Jaguar. Beamish of course saw him before Jack saw Beamish - no one got the drop on Beamish - and looked ahead as if he hadn't seen him. There he goes, thought Jack, the smug sod. Wonder what he's up to this afternoon?

Suddenly he wanted to *get Smiley*. No, don't get involved. Unethical. But the idea gave him pleasure. For years he'd told himself it was ethics kept him from going through the Reese and Smiley files to connect them. But he knew now with sick shame it was because he was terrified of what he might conclude. *Terrified* of Smiley. And he suspected the sod knew that, gloated on it. No, don't think about him. Leave well alone.

Jack got back to his office, took the lift up, and settled down to his correspondence. The lunch had been light, pea soup, half a bottle of red Sauvignon Kosher wine from Israel, and salt beef with cucumbers. His client had eaten nothing, he was too morose about the amount of money his wife was going to take him for.

You risked wife and business, all that, thought Jack, for a fuck with a bimbo in the back of your Roller.

Again he congratulated himself on not getting married. A bachelor. Like Smiley.

And it all came out again, didn't need to look up the files, his own, his father's and his grandfather's before him.

He shuddered as he recalled the mayhem over generations in Charnegate, involving Smiley's family, the Reeses. And poor Sam, that poor benighted chap.

Broken lives. Broken and charred bodies. And Smiley always there. With his red moppet-head of a mother said to have gone to America and not a dickie bird since.

Jack then did what he knew he must not do. He began to write down, with his steel-nibbed pen in clear script, all the

30

strange coincidences, wrote them down - would give it to the police. Not any policeman, an Inspector in Whitechapel he knew well. Just to read. Agreed anonymity. That would stir something up. *Get* Smiley. The pen scurried over the paper, only to leave for a stab at the inkwell.

At about four, Sheri, brought him a cup of tea. She was a mild mannered but highly efficient Indian girl, whose secretarial skills certainly deserved to be rewarded by more than Jack paid her. Jack did not notice the cooling tea. At five-thirty Shari left, leaving her boss to get on with locking up the office.

At 5.45 he was finished. He read it. He frowned. It was all circumstantial. There was nothing illegal to put on Smiley. It was all neat and tidy. Coroner's verdict on Sam's mother, Josie: "Accidental Death" He knew Smiley had been interviewed, but he could prove he was nowhere near the scene of the "accident"; that he was otherwise occupied.

He recalled his father, old Jack, had told him to treat Smiley as any other client. Old Jack kept stumpf: *Don't look under stones, just do your job.* (And anyway, where's the fee in all this?)

Jack shrugged, put a match to the document, and when it was consumed, methodically mashed the charred paper in his ashtray.

FORGET IT - but he'd keep a weather eye open on Sam, and that young girl Mae Fields.

Jack was just on his way out of the door when a beautiful woman, in a loose black overcoat of vicuna silk, met him on the landing. She was a head taller than he, and smelled of expensive perfume. He did not know one perfume from another, but he knew what was expensive, *this* was very expensive, and it seemed reminiscent of... he'd smelled it that very day, just a waft, and then he connected: Smiley vaporised scents like this, very faint, as if he had been stroking himself up against a perfumed woman. He dismissed the connexion, he didn't want Smiley's image to come between him and the enjoyment of the woman before him. 'What can I do for you?' he asked, because she was evidently seeking him out, his office was the uppermost in the building. She smiled showing teeth dazzling in their perfection. Nefertiti, he found himself thinking, she is more beautiful than Nefertiti. Like a perfect work of art. Reminded him of...? The mannequins in Nunnery, thirty years before.

Now he had a presentiment of danger so intense, he turned to run, but her hand shot out and grabbed him, easily drawing him to her, clawing into his shoulder. The yelp of pain never came out of his mouth, because she stifled it with her own mouth, her mouth on his. He felt his vitality ebb, smelt fish now, fish rotting, interwreathed with the smell of sewers, of freshly broken caskets of the dead, of cesspits rankly farting as bubbles burst.

She held him with one hand, swinging the plastic bag she carried as she delved into his pockets for his keys. She fished them out, held them up for him to see, 'Which key for the office, dog-shit?' The words were in his brain, her mouth still on his. He blinked hard, then very rapidly as she fingered the office key. She slid it in, and went in backwards, the plastic bag banging on the door jam, pulling Jack with her. With an abrupt flick of her left foot, she kicked the door shut. Inside the office there was a harsh yellow glare from the street lights.

He felt the scream coming and was glad, he would scream so loud the whole street would stop on hearing it. He would be rescued. He would escape. Again she filled his mouth with hers, again he felt his vitality ebb. She loosened the plastic bag - one of those cheap unmarked ones you get from small supermarkets - from her arm with a shrug so it fell to the floor.

With her right hand she grasped him by the nuts, and squeezed, sending white hot jolts of agony up his belly to the plexus, and up his spine to explode in his brain, and with the pain came the words, 'You know too much, you old fart. Just

32

look at you, a disgrace to the human race. Sooner or later you'd shop Beamish, stir it all up, envying his youth and vigour, while you age and dry up.'

Jack's face was wreathed up in stupefaction and pain, he hadn't uttered a sound, because she had her hand on his windpipe, and he had seen the nails sharpened to points, now they felt like claws and he felt the strength of the talon-like fingers. She could rip his windpipe out as easy as a child scoops spaghetti off a plate with a twirling fork.

She relaxed her hold on his testicles, (she could rip them off, Jack, rip them off, she has the strength of ten men), 'I wouldn't do anything, I swear it on my mother's grave, I wouldn't do anything.'

Susannah listened to his heart beating at 120 pumps a minute.

I'll suck the little toad's brain out through his nose, but now she detected his heart faltering.

She laid him out on his desk, easily keeping him still, one hand over his mouth pressing him down. With her other hand she unzipped his trousers, played around. Jack's pulse soared and kept on soaring, until first one, then another, of his brain arteries burst, closing down the brain. When she saw he was dead, she readjusted his dress and put him in his chair. His secretary would find him in the morning, an old man of seventy, dead of a fatal stroke.

Susannah changed into jeans, T-shirt and leather jacket from her plastic bag, then put her overcoat and dress into it.

Then she carefully rifled Regent's files, removing documents on the Reeses and Smileys, put them in her bag too.

She let herself out, letting the Yale lock click shut.

No one noticed the girl in jeans and jacket coming out of the building.

She was smiling to herself, thinking that when she told Beamish about how Jack Regent came to say goodbye to the world, he'd laugh himself sick.

With briskness, she walked back to Convent amongst the teeming rush hour crowds of East End, London.

CHAPTER EIGHT

Sam woke up feeling happy, but then realised that he was alone, there was only the warmth in the bed where Mae had slept. Then he recalled she had said she was going to be up early to finish some business at the hospital. He stumbled up, wanderingly made his way to the shower cubicle. The stream of hot water pounded on his skull like hailstones.

Being naked brought the old question: did it happen? Jacob said it was hallucination. A delusion. There was no proof either way. Often in life there never was proof of any kind, it was just a common consent that such and such was so, like, smoking was bad for you, that drunks die young, when the facts are often different. Some smokers lived well past the average age expectancy, and there were eighty year old drunks. But in this case it was one off, there was no common consensus. Here, it was like crossing against the traffic by yourself, you stood a good chance of being run down, even though you could see every car, whereas in a crowd waiting at the kerb, as soon as one person started to cross, the rest followed. Common consensus. You didn't even look at the traffic, and in the herd you were safe.

After five minutes under the faucet he was feeling a little more human. Even had an appetite, thought he'd go out to the working-men's cafe in Commercial Street and get himself a bacon sandwich, a real London bacon sandwich, thick greasy rashers on buttered bread cut from a whole loaf, larded with Heinz tomato ketchup, washed down with tea in a mug, thick sweet tea, so strong it was brown-red. Then he'd smoke a couple of Senior Service. Seemed like a good idea. But first his medication - five pills in all. He took them with water. Put the three phials back into the bathroom cabinet.

Absentmindedly, back in his bedroom, he pulled on his pair of Levis, which had genuine holes in the knees, not custom made, through years of kneeling in front of his clients as he pinned them up. Next he shrugged into a botany wool black pullover from Marks & Spencer's, and a pair of canvas trainers. He didn't trouble to comb his silver-white hair, which was getting very long now, but he did grasp the mane at the back, and do it ponytail with an elastic band. He needed a shave too, but the stubble was fashionably butch.

His anxiety hadn't totally dispelled as he finished dressing - it was just a delusion. But...

He got to the door, but as he opened it, there stood a tall, cheeky faced, big-bust blonde wearing high heels, no stockings, very short pink tube skirt and pink silk blouse, no bra, lots of cleavage.

'Hi, I'm Bella.' (He thought for a minute it was a kissagram.) 'I'm a friend of Mae's, she sent me over with your breakfast.'

A real honey of a girl. Didn't know Mae had a pal. But who else? Reminded him of one of Smiley's mannequins, the ones his father had in the display window downstairs, but this was a live one, with big Bristols. Could he be frightened of a girl? He was a big boy now.

She indicated the wickerwork basket she was carrying, in which he saw eggs in a carton, rashers of bacon, coffee, bread. 'Mae? You know Mae?'

'Who else? She wanted to surprise you.'

So she cooked him breakfast, he ate it with relish. She was waiting on him. He finished.

He knew he ought to get rid of her, but now he felt beholden. Then she struck at his good nature by saying, 'Will you make me a dress, Sam, measure me up for it?'

'Make you a dress,' he echoed, thinking her figure was a real and lovely challenge. She gave him no chance to argue, began to strip off, so, as she said, he could get the measurements proper.

He hesitated. She giggled, 'You shy?' No, he was thinking of Mae. Things were going too fast - but where was the harm, if Mae knew?

A slight crackling sound as the body electricity held onto her clothes as she stripped. Small tongues of bluish flame were just discernible as fibres came away from skin. Her clothes were off, she was wearing nothing but high-heeled shoes, and he was measuring her up.

They chatted as he worked. Seemed that Bella had known Mae when Mae worked as a makeup artist. Bella used to model, she said.

Within thirty minutes he had her covered in turquoise silk, held by pins, cut by shears, a beautiful design which showed every part of her to advantage.

Her body odour was like jasmine at first, but as she stood there, it gradually turned to roses, then lavender, but now it was fish like, no, he thought, more crab like, the smell you get when you boil a crab, a kind of warm sea breeze stench, or the waft from open baskets of cod. Smells that wriggle like eels. Then it changed again, a raw rutting stink that was so sharp he fancied it was scouring the mucous skin of the inside of his nose. Still fishy, it was rancid too, and he could not breath it in enough. It was like... like those few first seconds of his LSD trip, when your mind was still clear, but you could feel the nerve cells begin to vibrate. He breathed her in, his living nosegay. (A stab of fear - *that woman* smelt, the one that got him...) But this was just a cockney kid, and all women smelled. You couldn't have dressed as many women as he had without knowing a lot about female odours. Not one of the smells was new to him from her, it was common enough for a girl to sweat as she stood being fitted, so they would change their olfactory tang during the course of an hour.

'You like me, don't you Sam?'

He was standing up now. He lit a Senior Service, fumbled at his coffee cup, it was empty. She took it from him, and trailed over to the kitchen, returned with hot coffee in the cup. She was so easy to be with, he was really making her a nice dress, but her body odour was having a lulling effect on him. Maybe he had taken too many of his tranquillisers - or maybe not enough?

He really had no intention of making a pass at her, but she appeared so good-natured, so full of verve, so full of life, that he was relaxed with her, even though something told him at the back of his mind that he was playing with fire. He fixed his mind on the work, and on Mae, as he adjusted the fitting at her cleavage, and it was then she suddenly kissed him, slid her tongue into his mouth, apparently so artlessly, and that was all he remembered, for he fell into a deep sleep.

Bella got up from him, went to his office, found his diary. He was due to see a good half dozen people. He kept a meticulous diary, names and telephone numbers, and those he had not listed in his appointments, she found in his address book. She called them all, and got through to all but one to tell them their appointments were cancelled and Sam would get in touch. She made a note of the one she hadn't reached, that could be seen to later. It would be weeks before he was missed, really missed. That was all the time required. She then meticulously went round the premises turning off lights in the hallway, shutting windows, and then wrote out notes to be later affixed to the entrance cancelling milk (she had seen the bottles) and the morning papers. Beamish said he'd see to Mae.

The strange thing about a crowded city street is that it has tens of thousands of eyes, but the eyes are not used to see. You do not stare at people when you live in a city, you use your eyes to look away from their faces. The result is that everyone is invisible to everyone else. You are not seen. So no one saw the young woman with the brown nondescript coat and headscarf with the tall guy wearing jeans, trainers, and leather jacket. They came out of Sam's studio as it was getting dusk, and made their way to Convent, where Smiley let them in.

He came out of his walking coma just as Smiley pressed the button of the lift. He was too weak to do anything, except stand, looking at smiling Bella, feeling his throat on fire, a smell of fish in the air, a taste of fish in his mouth. Slime in his throat.

It was all happening again. No, just a flashback. But the doors of the lift are opening. Just what was waiting for him the other side?

CHAPTER NINE

What Sam was being forced into began many years before, when Tobias Smiley, Beamish's grandfather, an East End policeman, bought Convent for a song. No one else wanted the disused nunnery, it had a bad reputation - people said it was haunted - but Tobias was such a staunch Christian that a few old legends held no terrors for him. Newly married, he wanted space for the large family he planned, and thought too he could refurbish parts of the building for business letting.

Susannah was born to Daisy and Tobias Smiley on Good Friday, 1872. It was the same day of her mother's death (she was large, her mother small), leaving Tobias wondering what to do with Susannah, a flame-haired boisterous girl, so unlike his cockney- sparrow wife (both red-haired and green-eyed though). But he did not marry again, he was still in love with Daisy, built a memorial to her in Bethnal Green cemetery, which depicted a tall man embracing a young woman, which the monumental mason said was a depiction of an angel embracing a soul, which pleased Tobias mightily, and deepened his faith in Christ - the Resurrection promised to reunite Daisy to him. Yet he neglected Susannah, blaming her in his heart for his wife's death.

Not a Sunday would go by that he did not place flowers upon Daisy's grave, picking crocuses and later daffodils, in spring from Epping Forest, buying them at other times from Spitalfields traders. But he never took Susannah with him. She had to go to Sunday school, where they taught her she would go to hell unless she drank the blood of Christ; in hell you were tormented by devils, and there was fire and brimstone. When she heard that, she was on the side of devils from the start - Heaven was a boring place where you sang hymns all day long to a bearded brown-skinned god. (Besides, she had a secret.)

Susannah was so artful and mischievous that most weeks she would get a lashing from her father on her bare bottom. She submitted to him with a malicious, exquisite delight, as if sensing what it was doing to him.

Her father towered above her that day, Good Friday, 1884, her twelfth birthday. She'd been found out going down into the deep recesses of Convent, cellars and crypts which were out-of- bounds. He looked down, his face blotched with beer, his head spinning with a bout of grief for Daisy. 'This time you will never do it again, you young hussy! Take them off.'

Hiding her malevolent smirk, but she could not hide the flash of her emerald eyes, nor the reddening of her cheeks, she pulled up her skirt, and drew down her woollen drawers. The fire glittered metallically in the grate of the kitchen.

Tobias was praying to himself, *Spare the rod and spoil the child. Rightful is thine anger, Oh Lord, before the sins of the children. (Oh Daisy, if you were here now, this would not be happening.)*

He watched his daughter lie over the cleared kitchen table, her bottom on the edge, her buttocks rounded and spreading with beginning adolescence, her stocking half way up her thighs. She held the other edge of the table, and squeezed her eyes shut. His leather policeman's belt struck her hard, and a thrill of pleasure went through her body, spiralling up from her bottom, to between her legs, then her belly. He went on, and on, till she was screaming in delirium, pain and pleasure, abandonment and desire, alternating in feverish expectancy. She felt wet, and knew she had wet herself, as she always did, but this time Tobias had drawn blood.

Tobias blinked, as one coming out of trance, and there saw what he had done, the bruised flesh of his young daughter had broken, and was seeping blood down her legs.

'Dress yourself, and go to bed,' he ordered.

He then poured himself a beer from the frothing ewer, and looked into the hot coals of the fire. He did not turn to see his daughter go out of the room, which for his peace was just as well, for she was not sobbing any more, but squirmed into her pants, which lay around her ankles, looking defiantly at him, and then the look softened to one almost of pity: the pity of a panther who knows the rabbit cannot escape, a pity which does not prevent the kill.

Susannah went upstairs, and as she did so, she heard her father let in her uncle and aunt, Justin and Joan, Justin being her father's brother. She stopped on the stairs and listened, hearing that they were coming to live in Convent, where Justin would set up his tailor's shop.

Joan Smiley, née Stride, was twenty-eight, and had been married to Justin Smiley, the tailor, since she was sixteen.

Her family were drapers in Shoreditch, modest people, firm Christians, they never missed Sunday service at Christ Church, Spitalfields. It was at church she first saw Justin, a tall man, with unnaturally blonde hair, so blonde it was almost white. He had pale blue eyes and fine white teeth, though his mouth seemed too large. Yet when he smiled he could be charming. He was invariably dressed in black, and carried a silver topped cane. She felt his eyes on her throughout the service, and when she and her parents left, he was waiting outside the church for them. He raised his hat.

'Good morning Jonathan, and Mrs Stride,' he greeted, and she thought his voice was pleasing too, and he obviously knew her father. She was presented to him, and the following week he came to supper on the Sunday. They married a year later. They were so happy together, it seemed a fairy tale romance of a marriage.

Soon she was pregnant, but to her grief, the child, a girl, was stillborn. They might have got over that, but Justin and she moved into Convent, and there began her ambivalent relationship with her niece. Not that she had time to brood, because there was enough to do keeping the household running, making fires, shopping, cooking, keeping the house clean, and sometimes doing a little seamstressing for her husband's business. She read Jane Austin, and was learning Shakespeare's *Midsummer Night's Dream* by heart. She had few friends now, Convent seemed to enclose her in almost suffocating way.

Jonathan worked hard, for he was in his cutting room by seven every morning, well fed on kippers, or fried egg and bacon, washed down by a glass of Truman's beer. Joan was a good cook, and he always enjoyed the meals she made him. At ten she would bring him coffee in a large jug, with his Barbados sugar in a blue Wedgwood bowl, and a china mug with his initials painted on the side. Sometimes he would have a word with her, as he smoked a thin Dutch cheroot, then she would gracefully move away, to get on with her household tasks.

Most days, other than Sundays when they went to Christ Church, Spitalfields, followed similar patterns. He would open the showrooms at nine, and let his two young men sales assistants in. At twelve he lunched with Joan in the kitchen: a pork chop on Mondays, potatoes, cabbage, followed by one of her puddings - she made a marvellous spotted-dick - all washed down by beer. He would see his clients in the afternoon, measure or fit them, then he could shut up shop at six, read the *Daily Telegraph* as he smoked his cherrywood pipe, filled with Virginia tobacco, relaxing with a glass of porter in the drawing room. Dinner was seven sharp, served on the blue and gold Wedgwood dinner set, when the whole family, the two brothers, Joan, and her niece Susannah, would eat.

Oddly though, there were no maids, even though they could afford one. Somehow, the few who had been hired soon left, and though this dispirited Joan, Susannah was happy about it, and did more than her share of household chores.

After dinner Tobias and Justin would play chess, and the women would embroider. Bed was at ten, and Justin always liked to watch Joan dress, or rather undress, for bed.

He knew she was nervous of him, now that they had tried so hard to have another child, and Susannah 's potions of herbs from Epping Forest didn't seem to help. His habit was to make love to her after she fell asleep, that way there was less trouble from her because she could pretend to be asleep, though he knew when he'd woken her from her slumber by his hard rhythmic thrusting into her soft flesh. Nowadays he often took a long time to climax. He was however not in two minds about that side of his marriage, he did not intend to change anything there. No, that would go on, after all she was his wife, and it was her duty to submit to him. In any case, women weren't supposed to gain pleasure - but he suspected that teasing little minx of a niece of his would take pleasure, not knowing she would often be outside their bedroom door, smiling to herself as she listened to him.

CHAPTER TEN

Tobias looked up from feeding his chickens as his brother's shadow fell over him. Tobias was a tall man for those days, fully six-two and two hundred pounds, he was thirty pounds heavier than his brother, who stood an elegant five-ten. People who didn't know them always mistook Tobias for the elder brother, but he was younger by a year, a fine looking man with mutton chop whiskers, and a fine head of hair so blonde it was white, a Smiley characteristic. His eyes too were like his brother's, very pale pastel blue irises. He smiled, 'Care for a drink?'

Justin, his face worried, looked at the chickens, fascinated by their powerful beaks, as they pecked at the Norfolk corn Tobias fed them. The flock was Rhode Island Red, some two baker's dozen, with one tall dandycock, whose red plumage was gold at the breast, and black of wing, gold of sprightly tail feathers. His wattle was intense red, and Justin turned away, the richly vascularised tissue reminded him too much of... he didn't want to put the word to it. He turned to his brother, noting the size ten feet in workingmen's iron shod boots, the corduroy trousers, brown and worn at the knees, the white shirt without collar and the black waistcoat. He'd cut all his brother's clothes, and he was a fine advertisement in his dress police uniform, even finer in his Sunday suit of black serge. The women of Spitalfields always cocked an eye at Sergeant Tobias Smiley, finest figure of a man hereabouts, and there were some dandy ones to be seen. Justin looked him in the eye, 'How's Susannah?'

Tobias threw the remaining handful of corn to his appreciative chickens who had been cluttering and clucking around his boots, watched by the cockerel, concerned about his male supremacy. 'She's her own mistress,' he said bleakly, then dismissed the subject. 'We'll wet our beaks, it'll be just right to taste.' He meant the Truman beer.

They went into the kitchen and in the event, they had some Cheshire cheese with their draught, and thick wedges of bread.

They sat in silence at the table. Susannah cut them bread, gave Justin a lovely smile. Tobias knew he'd come to gawp at her. Even though he has his own suite of rooms with Joan, he was for ever coming down and sniffing about, it was becoming a habit. It didn't bode well.

Tobias offered him more beer, which he greedily accepted, 'How's Joan today?'

'Well, brother, she is well. A keen churchwoman, hope it gives her peace.'

Tobias had watched her the day before, shopping in Spitalfields, she had a faraway look in her eyes. He noticed she was walking in a strange mechanical way, as if her joints were stiff. And she such a young woman. Tobias leered, who would have thought Justin was so demanding? He caught himself in his male thinking, supposing he was wrong about that, the bloody fool was too busy thinking about Susannah, but then, maybe he was always thinking about her, and his wife just came in handy. It wasn't a pretty idea, and he sometimes wished that Justin hadn't come to Convent, for his marriage's sake. They had been so happy before.

'Well,' said Justin, 'I'll be back to work.' But he was still looking at Susannah, noting her fine lines, her very attractive figure as she worked at the sink, and decided he would have to do something more than moon about this girl.

Tobias and he exchanged a few more words, and then Justin left.

He looked at Susannah and she stared back, eyes garnet sharp, then got on with making one of her potions without a word.

Tobias turned away.

The girl was beyond his control, with her alchemies and her helping the local women in god knows what female

46

secrets. Best leave it alone, like all wise men since time began. There was no question of beating her any more, no question, God knows what she might do. Those hard eyes of hers made the message plain. Leave well alone. He'd got the message, and besides, she was good to him when he didn't interfere.

Tobias awoke to hear Susannah grunting and groaning with mounting excitement. He had heard that sound before, it was the sound of his wife as he pleasured her. He put his hands to his ears, but the rutting continued till he could stand it no more. Angrily, he got out of bed and went to his daughter's bedroom. He turned up the gas to reveal her writhing on the bed in sexual heat, her legs splayed wide, her hair flaming over the pillow, her breasts taut.

Tobias felt afraid, he wanted to shake his daughter by the arm, awaken her, but he feared touching her ever since the whipping. So he turned away and went downstairs. The sounds became fainter the further he got from the room, until in the kitchen he could hear nothing. He drank a brandy, lit his pipe, sat before the dying fire, looked at the embers, now deepening as they consumed the fresh air his entrance had caused to sweep into the room. He thought despite himself of his nubile daughter. He cursed her under his breath, his wife had died giving birth to her, she was bad blood, damn her.

Susannah looked out over the gravestones in the Convent cemetery. There was fog on the grass, and mist hung low, creeping over the tombstones.

She liked to go down into the crypt, where she felt better, though both her father and her auntie Joan tried to stop her now. But she would go, she would, no matter what they said. Besides, they didn't really know where she went, true she went down to the crypt, but she went even further than that. And it was much better there.

Justin knew Susannah prowled around the unused parts of the building, was especially fond of Crypt. Why?

He held the keys tightly in his hand, descended the stone steps beneath the ground floor. He also had a lantern. At first, he was hoping to find Susannah.

The crypt was high ceilinged, vaulted, with huge flagstones for the floor, it was some forty feet by forty, and at the northern end was another church door, and finding the right key, Justin unlocked it, and was surprised how easily the lock moved. He was careful on the steps, for they seemed a trifle damp, but soon, spiralling anticlockwise, down the steps, he was in very large space, some fifty by forty, and with a ceiling height of about fifteen feet. There were numerous pillars to support the building above.

There was another door, no doubt it would lead downward even further, he tried the keys, but none fitted. He shrugged, was about to go back up the stairs, when he felt a chill, and unaccountably he thought of Susannah. She was growing fast, no longer a child.

The idea made him randy, so he went back up to his wife, the tall, stately, brunette, who had yet to conceive again.

The years passed uneventfully, except that of default, for Joan never did get pregnant, and she took more of an interest in her fey niece Susannah, but it was Justin who had an even stronger interest, and it was becoming an obsession.

He decided to make her a red silk dress, just for her, a secret between them.

He was drawn to Crypt, again and again, though he tried to keep away, then one day, when Susannah was uppermost in his mind, he went to the crypt, and this time he found the door he had never opened, ajar. He descended the stair, deep into the bowels of the earth, not knowing this was where Susannah came.

He was unprepared for the hideous sickening blast of cold air that assailed him. Worse, he thought, than a dosshouse, but it cleared, so he continued down the anticlockwise spiral stone stairs. Now he smelt another odour, offish, of fish, mingled with the perfume of rich, ripe, roses.

By now he was in the lower chamber, a large room, but smaller than the two above, with huge grey flat stones cladding the walls, and vaulting from pillars supporting the slightly domed roof. There was nothing before him, merely flagstones, and the walls, then he turned round, and cried out in terror, nearly dropping his lantern - there was a pit yawning beneath him.

Another smell was coming out of the pit. It came up in a cold stream, like a slithering serpent, enveloping him, coiling about him. It was intoxicating and foul, beautiful and horrid, soothing and disgusting. It made him feel in rut, and he understood why dogs in spring will roll and lie in rotting meat or vile refuse, their legs sticking up in the air, a ferocious grin of pleasure on their jaws, pink tongue lolling out. He'd seen even spaniels do it, but the one he recalled in Bethnal Green had been a white bull terrier, squirming on a rotting, maggot-infested carcass of a ginger cat run over by the iron shod wheels of a brewery wagon.

'This must be the gape of the lime pit,' he whistled, 'the one they used to fill with bodies in the 1665 plague. His voice echoing dully, 'there must be thousands of corpses down there, and rats.'

He shuddered, was Susannah coming down here? He pictured her attractive form, staring into the pit. Then he effortlessly pictured her naked, saw every line of her, every curve and dimple, even to her most private self.

He would have to possess her.

A day or so later Susannah was standing by the pit, but all she could smell was fresh perfume, the scents of pomegranates, incense, myrrh and frankincense. She could hear flutes, and saw beautiful girls in silk gowns dance in long swaying lines. How silly the girls at school had been who said she had such an imagination when she had told them about this place, but she soon learned not to tell them her secrets, and they were wise enough not to bother her, because they feared she might do something to them. Well, that was some time ago, she had outgrown them, just as she had laughed in her teacher's face when she left, calling her a dried up old bag for always telling tales to her father on how mischievous she was in class. She didn't care about any of them, nor the people she lived with.

Her friend came towards her, so stately, every inch a priestess, so gracious, with pale olive skin and dark hair. She had emeralds to Her long slender neck, a silk blouse of white and gold stripe, a shawl of purple silk about her shoulders. On Her long slender hands were amethysts and rubies. She smelt of pomegranates, of myrrh, of frankincense, of crushed flowers. Her eyes were wide and blue, full of life, Her nose aquiline, slightly hawked, oh, so slightly, Her mouth a rich ruby, with full sensuous lips, which smiled revealing perfect teeth and pink tongue. Upon her large but beautifully formed ears there hung pearls arranged in silver droplets. Her voice was low, melodious, just the kind of voice Susannah wanted to hear, just as her friend looked exactly as she wanted to see. As if this could be her imagination!

Her friend told her all sorts of things, no one else ever spoke about. Explained what her uncle Justin wanted, and how her father was all mixed up in himself, like every other man, about sex, and how they would be punished for it.

It was so good to be down here in Crypt, by the pit, here she was never alone. All she ever wished for came true here.

Susannah knelt down, the Lady stood over her. How well She smelt. She pulled her to her belly, and it was wonderful, so soft, so warm, so alive. Then she raised her up, and kissed her on the mouth. Delicious pulsations of pleasure coiled from her lips to her breasts, to her belly, to the heart of her.

Susannah kissed her hands, then left, but she did not leave a foul smelling empty dungeon, with a reeking pit at its centre, but the courtyard of a priestess' house; she was not a lonely girl, but the confident of someone so much more wonderful than anyone in the whole wide world.

CHAPTER ELEVEN

Justin spent a fairish sum on the silk, and lavished time, care and skill on the dress for Susannah. Carrying the scarlet creation to her when her father was pounding the beat, and his wife was out shopping in Spitalfields Market, Justin found her in the kitchen dicing beef.

'I've got something for you,' he announced archly, holding the present behind his back. Wash your hands, and see!'

When she turned around from the sink after flushing blood from her hands, she saw the shimmer garment, full length, hanging from Justin's arms. 'Strewth, Justin, it's beautiful, and no mistake.'

Before he could say anything more, she was shucking out of her work blouse and skirt, revealing her very full figure. In a trice she had the dress on. 'How do I look?'

Justin choked, 'Like a goddess.'

He could not stop himself, he was up to her, embracing her, but the look in her bright green eyes forewarned him not to go any further.

'I burn for you,' he breathed, 'burn.'

She laughed, 'Keep the fires stoked, Justin, you won't wait in vain.'

She said it in such a way that he was full of hope, and he reflected, there was an odd kind of pleasure in the pain of waiting, knowing he would get what he wanted.

When this very young woman was ready.

Throughout the misery of her barren marriage and Justin's careless, brutal use of her, Joan enjoyed one great solace, her niece Susannah. True, it had been sickening the way he fawned on the girl, taking her out for walks in Victoria Park, even special jaunts to the Serpentine in Hyde Park, but Susannah had always been careful not to rub her nose in it (was that worse?) and really the fault was all his, he being a mature man, and she just a girl. Now, with such disappointments, that all seemed rather small fry in her loneliness, a loneliness which Susannah not only seemed to understand, but could in some magical way alleviate, even just by being with her. Of late though, she wasn't merely being with her, but was attentive and reassuring.

'Let me comb and brush your hair, Joan. It is so pretty, reminds me of a friend of mine, hair blue-black like a raven's wing down at the Tower of London.'

Joan would sit and watch herself in a hand mirror as Susannah brushed her hair.

'That's a pretty song,' Joan said one day, 'I have never heard it before. What does it mean?'

Susannah shook her head to suggest she didn't know, and sang a verse again. 'Lady of the white tower, gold and silver at your feet, kiss the carmine flower, for your beauty to complete.'

'Sad and lovely,' said Joan.

Susannah smiled a smile of knowing a secret.

Susannah woke to the full moon and got out of bed, running her fingers along the wall of the corridor to find her father's bedroom. Noiselessly she opened his door, and saw him lying with the gas lamp on, on his back, deep asleep. Or was he feigning sleep? it didn't matter, he wouldn't dare to face the truth. That he knew what was happening as she pulled the sheets from him, and straddled him with her young strong legs. His seed spurted into her belly once, twice, three pulses, and all the while his eye were shut. Then she left him, and went back to her room.

She only did it for her friend.

Susannah waited until she was sure she was pregnant, three whole months, and then it was time for Justin, who was drinking beer in the kitchen, her father out on the beat as usual.

She wore the red dress he had made for her.

He looked up, ravished by her vitality, her musky scent.

'It's time, Justin, we'll go upstairs. In your bed.'

'But Joan is there.'

'Don't worry, she'll be asleep - she'll think it all a dream.'

Joan saw them come into the bedroom, as she lay like a statue, her long body swathed in a white lace nightie. She watched as they took their clothes off and got into bed with her, but she could not say anything, could not move. It was like a nightmare, where you try to speak, but cannot, try to run, but your legs will not obey you.

'Now, Justin. Now!'

As if mesmerised, Joan understood, but could not act. Knew that her niece was wantonly opening her legs.

Joan wanted to scream, but could not open her mouth, nor shut her eyes, nor move a limb. It must be a dream, but she knew it was not. In her panic, a panic of total stock stillness, she felt as if her body was no longer hers to control; oddly in her torment, the gas lights seemed to pacify her, their colours not merely pearl-like, but all hues of the rainbow. But it was not a peaceful sensation overall, since the most marked feeling she had was of being buried alive, buried in a new kind of body, a body which was somehow angry, and delirious, eager to consume - what?

Justin was available.

Joan's eyes brightened, glowed in the dull light of the gas lit bedroom - at least that had returned to normal. She was watching Justin, all control gone, completely used as she wished by Susannah. Joan saw his eyes dilate, bulge, then shrink back into their sockets. All the while Susannah held him tight, her mouth forced up against his.

Joan writhed, until with a sudden sound of scale upon scale, as when serpents intertwine, or metal on metal is gently scraped, Joan sat up and grabbed him, forced him between her legs.

Later that night, a tall woman with a shawl over her head pulled tight about her features, stood in the shadows of Dorset Street outside the biggest doss house. She knew a woman would come out, sooner or later, of Joan's height and age, and she knew what to do when that happened. At twelve midnight, by the clock on Christ Church, a woman did, she was Nan Reese, white-skinned and dark-haired, widowed and without children, young, like the woman watching her.

Nan looked into her purse, by the gas light, and the glum expression she wore told of little largesse to be found. She wanted a drink, and she needed money to stay at the doss house. There was only one way to get it. She made her way to the Britannia pub at Crispen Corner.

The tall woman watched, then fell in step behind her. Yes, she was the right build, the right height, the right age. The tall woman came by, the fog swirling before them, the cobblestones gleaming, 'Filthy sort o' night, dear,' she said, and Nan responded without breaking her stride to look at her. She felt no alarm - after all, the stranger was a woman, 'It is and no mistake,' she agreed.

'Needs a warm noggin in the belly on such a night as this.'

'We'll be going to the Britannia?' asked Nan expectantly.

'Aye, later,' the tall woman replied, 'I does for a gent nearby. Got to check the fire. Come on in with me.'

She did. No one saw them going into Convent. An hour later, Nan had revealed to the woman that though she had relatives, no one bothered much about her, and no one was expecting to see her for some time. The doss house. Bed was sixpence, and that was what she, and 50,000 others, charged for herself. She had lodged at Dorset Street for some weeks now, and hoped to get out of the "life".

There was nothing to be alarmed at - the woman said she could help her clean up, besides, what was Christian charity for? Nan had heard rumours about Convent, but on a cold night, it was hardly surprising that she would take up the offer of warmth, food, and perhaps a few pence. Besides, the woman was so pleasant to be with.

There was a fire in the grate of the kitchen, cheese on the table, bread, and luxury of luxuries, red wine. The woman, whom Nan learned to call Susie, poured her generous potions, until poor Nan was out on her feet. She did not respond or complain when she felt herself being helped across the floor, 'We'll put you to bed, for a snooze, Nan, and you'll be right as rain. Wine makes you sleepy when you aren't used to it.' Susie was remarkably strong, easily helping her up the stairs, and my, it was bliss to fall upon the bed. (What was that shape in the shadows on the floor? An old dress? A pile of clothes?) Oh, it was bliss in this sweet smelling bed. What were the smells? Let me count the smells. Lavender, roses, lime - and the smell of love, of love. It made her wrinkle her nose in delight.

Then she felt the pillow over her face, and though she was big and strong, she could not push it from her. Above her, Susannah pressed down with all her might until the kickings stopped.

She was peaceful in death, with no bleeding, no trickle from nose or mouth, even her colour was merely that of a flushed drinker. Susannah went through her pockets, taking all the incombustibles. Take rings from her fingers, and bells from her toes, she giggled. These were to be thrown into the Pit. She then stripped Nan and dressed her in Joan's nightie. Laying Justin there was not easy, he was in a tight ball, his head pulled against his knees, his teeth white and grinning from his emaciated skull. He was so tightly sprung up, it was difficult even with her strength, so she got a meat knife from the kitchen and hacked at the tendons of his wrists until the fingers uncoiled. There was no blood. She soon unrolled him after that, and stripped him, putting his clothes in the closet. My, what a pretty young pair they made together in the bed, she thought. She took Nan's clothes downstairs and began to feed the fire, a piece at a time, to be consumed without trace, as long as she kept stoking the coals.

Satisfied, she went back to the dead pair, and set fire to the bed in several places with a large sulphur kitchen match. Joan's perfume help to make the bed sheets more flammable. She almost forgot, then put Joan's wedding ring on Nan's marriage finger. She watched the scene, saw the fire would take hold, and was glad dear Papa was out pounding the beat.

Now the flames were crackling fiercely.

She began to laugh as she raced downstairs to Crypt to see Joan. Shortly after, she rushed from Convent, wearing her nightgown, into Commercial Street, shouting, 'Fire!'

CHAPTER TWELVE

Susannah, of course, did not care a fig that she was unmarried and pregnant, but it was prudent to be married, so as to avert any curiosity about her. She was already well known in Charnegate, as a real friend in need to any of the women in the neighbourhood. And she was not short of suitors.

The man Susannah married for propriety before the birth of her son, was Jarvis Whistle. He was not so tall as Tobias, but a bit broader. He had thick naturally curly hair, a pleasant, undistinguished face with a weak mouth eclipsed by a walrus moustache. His eyes were small, deep set, his complexion florid. His parents were modest folk, running a tobacconists in Bethnal Green.

His main attraction to Susannah was his availability, he was her father's constable. Tobias liked Jarivs because he could always beat him at chess. Off duty, they would often go back to Convent and have a few pints and a game.

Jarvis watched Susannah grow from a gangly girl to a young woman. He was smitten - Susannah was tall, white-skinned, and luscious. She had a full figure, and a head of lovely dark red hair which fell in sweeping curls, white, white teeth which showed when she laughed, a harsh, thrilling laugh, she showed them to the gum, and they appeared ravenous. He saw even this as something to be lauded, it showed her strength, and because he was such a strapping man, he had to have a strapping wife. Then there were her hands, they were tipped with strong nails, almost bluish in colour, and she filed them to points. He wondered why, but dare not ask.

Seeing that she laughed at his jokes, stood close to him when he was saying his farewells, and in general conveyed to him she favoured him, even to the extent sometimes of giving him the best pork chop from the platter when he came for lunch, he sought to speak to her of things of the heart. How to do it? It would be unseemly for her to meet him alone, but until he had some real indication of what her thoughts of him were, he could hardly go to Tobias and ask his permission to walk his daughter out. He solved the problem by going to church with them. He manoeuvred that she would be between him and Tobias. When they were kneeling in prayer and the vicar was intoning, Tobias would be quite rent with religious exultation, and did not notice that his daughter and Constable Whistle were whispering together.

'Yes, of course you can ask him if you can walk me out,' she said with a delicious smile, moving closer to him, so he could smell her fragrance. What was that perfume? She smelt of crushed flowers, of seeds bursting open, of poppies pressed to the lips, of ripening grain. He could smell flowers, but the people round them were becoming restless, agitated, for they could smell a reeking corpse, and then the stench passed. As for Tobias, he was long used now to the odours that came when his daughter was near.

'So you'd like to take Susannah out, would you, cock?' Tobias asked rhetorically after lunch that day, when the two of them were in the sitting room, and Susannah was clearing away the dishes.

'I would an' all.'

'Think you can handle her then?'

'Handle her?'

'Aye, handle her. She is more than a handful, and has a stubborn streak to her, But she's good at the oven, as well you know, and tidy round the house. No one can hold a candle to her when it comes to haggling with them damned street traders. Sharp as a razor.'

'A fine figure of a woman,' was all he allowed himself, but Tobias continued, 'They call them the weaker sex, but let me tell you, as a widower, and father of Susannah, that women the likes of her are stronger than any man. People fear and love her, you know that, don't you, Jarvis? She is the best midwife ever to be in these parts, and the women swear by her. They will go to labour with her and her alone, not wanting a doctor. I have heard she has wonderful skills, some say magical, with herbs from Epping Forest.' (Aye, he thought to himself, it's not only the birthings they call her for. Women's ways, not for men to question.) 'But then, we men, what are we in the procreative process? Just the seed makers, that is all, just the seed. You cannot be sure who the father of any child is, but there can never be any doubt as to its mother.'

'I'll do my best,' said Jarvis, bemused.

'I would like grandchildren,' Tobias went on, 'a joy for my old age.' Tobias refilled their glasses, 'Let's drink to your marriage, and that it may be fruitful.'

'Amen to that.' So it would go apace. Just as well, he could hardly wait.

Susannah urged him on, and much mirth it gave her too. Within the week, there was the set piece of the popping of the question, which occurred in the parlour, before the fire. She replied, 'Jarvis Whistle, you are not on your knee.' He reddened, but seeing that though she was smiling - those teeth! - that she was not joking, dutifully performed. He knelt before her, while she sat on the plush settee. He was near swooning with lust, love, and passion for her. The reeking smells that came from her were richer more redolent that ever. He snudged his nose appreciatively.

Susannah cocked her head as if listening. She smiled and said, 'Yes.'

...an itching, a sore itching, then flaming petals of (pink flowers?) heat radiating from her womanhood, out, into her belly - she was hungry...

Dressed like a street drab, with a shawl to hide her beautiful head of black hair, she left Convent late at night, and no one saw her except Susannah who beckoned her out into Cripple Way when she saw the street was clear.

They smiled at one another. 'Temple Hire,' said the dark haired woman, referring to the old practice of priestesses in Babylon.

'Temple Hire,' Susannah whispered back. She waited, and then, with her shopping basked under her arm, her belly huge with pregnancy, jauntily walked back to Convent.

As Joan plied her ancient trade, Susannah give birth.

Susannah's son Beamish was a beautiful child, perfect in every part of him, a large boy of some eight pounds. He was born with a caul, which Susannah herself peeled away. Pale blue eyes looked back at her, as and she put him to her breast. Of course she had no midwife, she just squatted down on the floor when her time came, and caught the child. She did not bite through the umbilicus, the serpent of life, until Beamish had been breathing for thirteen minutes, thereby avoiding the residual brain damage that modern babies have when the cord is cut immediately on delivery and the mother is trussed up like a torture victim. Then they smack its back to make it breathe. Susannah knew nothing of this cruelty, only what her Lady told her to do, to look into her ancestral mind, to look deep in herself and find what the truth of her being was.

The maid would come for the afterbirth, and the pail of waters, and they would be buried in the garden, where the chickens scratched in the rich soil of what had once been part of the Convent cemetery.

As for Jarvis, he wondered about the quickness of the pregnancy, some three months short, but then his mates dug him in the ribs and congratulated him on getting his leg over a fine wench like Susannah, and to tell the truth, he wouldn't want to spoil that reputation. But... who was it ? Why you, Susannah told him, you my dearest, when we used to canoodle, don't you remember? He did and he didn't, but for the while it was easier to take the compliments.

As Beamish grew, he would not obey anyone but his mother; he did what his grandfather told him to, but only in those areas she said he should. When something new cropped up, Beamish would run to her and ask if he had to do as Tobias said. On things religious, Tobias had no remit whatsoever. If he did try to talk about the Bible, Beamish would cover up his ears and start to scream. As for Jarvis, he could not control the boy at all, indeed Beamish was openly contemptuous of him.

At first it had been wonderful with Susannah, she was passionate and willing, but she got pregnant so quickly, he was not allowed near her after the first week. Since then she sometimes let him have her, but only during Easter and Lent. He once tried to force her. She'd looked him straight in the eyes and said, 'You still have a chance, Jarvis, to remain a whole man, if you let me go now. Hold me any longer than the laugh in my throat, and I will unman you.' He let her go. His blood ran cold. He never tried again. Would never try again.

Besides, she wasn't all bad to him, there were the anniversaries, and sometimes when she was feeling especially good, usually on a full moon, she would lull him to sleep with her fingers. It was like - he had no words for it. It was heaven, yes, heaven. She seemed to know when to do it, for she sensed his tension, and relieved him. He was deeply in love with her most of the time, but when he realised how in thrall he was to her, he drank.

Jarvis snored in the kitchen, Good Friday afternoon, 1896. Drunk now, his paunch swelled tight as the pigskin on a drum, curved and hairless it strained out of his cotton shirt.

He awoke and saw Beamish looking at him with pale blue eyes. Jarvis looked back, and was mesmerised by the intense hatred in the boy's expression. Neither of them moved. The kitchen was sultry, because it was warm, and because the cooking fire was glowing. Flies buzzed over the plate of raw meat, others died noisily on the arsenic-laced fly papers, that hung in ugly grey green spirals from the gas lamp brackets.

Outside, Tobias was looking at his chickens, which were listlessly picking at the grain he fed them.

In the scullery, Susannah was washing underclothes, her own, and her son's, but today she wasn't going to do her husband's filthy underpants, nor her father's. She would put them back, neatly folded - unwashed - in their cupboards, and they would wear them as they had been doing for the past month, too terrified of her to say anything.

Jarvis was still looking at his son, except he knew Beamish was not his natural son at all. There could not be a son of his loins who would look at him with such utter naked fury and disgust as this little sod. But whose son? No, it was unthinkable. Besides, she was a virgin on their wedding night, of that he was sure, because she had bled. (Of course she had, she put a chicken liver there, a slice, and it did the trick.)

Beamish was stock still, his shirt spotless, white and well ironed, his short flannel trousers above his white knees, his long socks unwrinkled, his little black shoes beautifully polished. His hair was perfectly brushed and parted on the left, hair of a silky white, face a muddy milk colour, mouth blood red, lips large, pendulous.

Beamish poked his tongue out at him. Jarvis swung out his arm to strike him, his fist clenched, but Beamish stepped back with astonishing agility, easily dodging the blow. Jarvis stood up. Beamish squinted his eyes, daring him to do it again, mocking him. Jarvis, struck out again, and this time he could have sworn the boy let himself be hit, his huge fist caught him a crack on the skull. There was a sickening sound as fist and skull connected, a sound of fluids being whooshed in a jug, Beamish yelled a shriek of pain, and fell headlong against the heavy kitchen table, blood gushing out of his nose and ears.

Susannah bounded into the kitchen so quickly that she saw her son crashing into the table as Jarvis raised his fist again. Her face blanched, she picked up her father's knife and went for him.

Tobias, alerted by Beamish's cry, came in behind them. Sizing up the situation, he felled Jarvis with a sledgehammer blow to the back of his head.

Jarvis uttered a short snarl of a cry and plunged forward, his arms outstretched. Susannah stepped to the side and let him fall to the ground, hearing with satisfaction the smash of his nose, and the crack of his teeth against the large kitchen floor tiles. Casting a quick look of gratitude to her father, she tended her son, who though bloodied, was recovering consciousness quickly.

She cradled him in her arms, rocking him from side to side, 'Oh my poor baby, my poor baby.' Beamish snuggled up against her large bosom, feeling happier than he ever had before. Mama loved him. 'Of course, my little prince, of course I love you.'

Tobias looked at the touching pair, tears coming to his eyes. There was guilt too, because he knew he had kept love from her himself. He put out his huge hand, which was turning blue from the blow he had given his son-in-law, and touched her head. 'Is the boy all right, is he all right?'

Susannah looked up, reacting to his grave concern, and nodded, but she was far from sure.

You must let him walk after concussion.

Abruptly she stood up, and taking Beamish by the hand, walked out into the garden, glad that the bleeding had stopped.

Are you feeling better, she asked, without opening her mouth. He nodded, but there was still terror in his eyes. She felt murder rise in her heart at what Jarvis had done. *He must go.*

Yes, and rather sooner than otherwise he would have.

CHAPTER THIRTEEN

Jarvis scrambled up from the kitchen floor, put his hand to his mouth, felt teeth shards and blood with spittle on his lips, went to the sink and turned the brass tap on, put his head under the cascade, gasping for air, as he could not breath through his smashed nose. He spat out broken teeth, and gobbets of blood. He was florid with pain and anger. He could hear Susannah crooning outside and thought to go out there and beat her to a bloody pulp. Then he was aware of Tobias by his side. Involuntarily, he cringed from the older and taller man.

Tobias spoke close to his ear, 'Thee touch the lad again or hurt Susannah, and I'll swing for 'ee, Jarvis. Mark my words, before God, I will.'

Sullenly, Jarvis backed away, pulled his coat from the chair, a nice tweed as he was off duty, put his Derby hat on, and left, silently vowing never to return.

He was some distance from the house, walking along Cripple Way to Commercial Street, when to his utter astonishment, Susannah pattered past him, stood afront him, a look of anguished concern on her mobile features.

'Oh, love,' she said in a low and sweet voice, her hands clasped to her throat, her red dress lurid in the dying sunlight, 'your poor face. Come on in, and let me bathe it for you.'

A stifled gasp came from his bloodied mouth. He wanted to curse her, to reject her, but he couldn't find the words, instead he sobbed.

She embraced him about the neck so he could smell that heady perfume of her, smells of roses and lilac, the smell of a healthy woman, clean and needing. She drew closer so he could feel her softness against him, her breasts full and squashed up against his chest. 'There, there, there, love,' she was saying, 'There, There.' She was promising him comfort, loving care, and after, there would be her body. It was Easter. She led him back by the hand.

He sat on an ash kitchen chair, one made in Whitechapel, as his wife bathed his face. 'Would you like a drink of beer?' Susannah asked, coaxingly, 'Perhaps a noggin of brandy?'

He nodded.

'I'll join you, love. I know you didn't mean to hurt the boy.' She continued to lie to him, and he enjoyed it, it was so sweet to believe.

She came to him later that day, as evening was reddening the sky, came into their bedroom, and undressed before his longing gaze, then she drew the bed clothes from him. He breathed her smell in, ruttish and sharp, of sex and womanliness. True his face still hurt, but the brandy dulled the pain, while she and it fired his passion. He had never known her so complaisant.

Below, in his narrow bed, Beamish heard him grunt and hated him, hated him.

In the kitchen, Tobias heard the creak of the bed, and hated him too, thinking him a drunken no good, who would soon have to be thrown out of the police force.

What's happening now, Tobias wondered, there's no more noise from the bed, instead there was a kind of whimpering, a sort of sobbing, and was that laughter, Susannah's laughter following a sudden shriek of pain from Jarvis? And whose footsteps had he heard a little earlier outside in the hall, going past his door? Must have been Susannah. Must have.

Well, well, leave well alone, he concluded, mustn't come between man and wife. With that conclusion he turned over in bed and fell fast asleep.

Dr Hildegard wore a frockcoat and a top hat, one of the old school. He was past seventy years of age, but was spry, his goatee beard still had black hairs in it, and his monocle accentuated the brightness of his eyes. He stood by the bed looking down at Jarvis, whose expression was pleading, as if he wanted to say something. 'Been like this a week, you say?' Hildegard snapped. He looked up, Tobias and Susannah (Deuce, she looked grief-stricken, observed Hildegard) were at the other side of the bed. They nodded in unison.

Tobias said, 'He's been paralysed and mute for a week, but he's shrunk since then.'

'Shrunk?' fired the good doctor, still counting Jarvis's pulse. It was a thin straggling pulse, very low.

'I estimate he's lost fifty pounds,' Tobias said.

Hildegard sniffed, must have been the deuce of a fever. He's sallow too. Could be a touch of jaundice - but the paralysis? He did not know what that might be. He knew him to be a heavy drinker. The symptoms would pass as he dried out...

'Feed him plenty of Scotch broth, lots of fluids, and he may have a pint of beer twice a day.'

With that economy of dissertation, Hildegard snapped his watch shut, put it into his waistcoat pocket, and took up his bag. Tobias led him downstairs, and paid his fee, a hefty guinea. Meanwhile Susannah was crooning, *'Ring a ring o' roses... atishoo, atishoo, we all fall down.'*

It was the plague song, sung after the Bubonic Plague in London, unaccountably today a nursery tune.

All Jarvis could see was a woman, the most beautiful he had ever seen. She gave off an odour at once repellent and exciting, like Susannah. But there were other smells too. Of crushed fruit in Whitechapel Road, of beer long standing in the glass, of rut, of sweat, of perfumes so tantalising. Yet there was more, there was the smell of death, but this time it was his death, and he knew it was as Joan bent over him, opened her silk gown, then slid her tongue into his mouth.

He gagged, struggled, to no avail. She pinioned him with her arm so easily, and her tongue ripped him like a razor,

67

digging deeper into his soft tissues. He bit at her tongue but made no impression.

Laughing, she turned him over, spread his legs, impaled him with her arm up to his liver, then fell on him again, poking out his eyes with her tongue, and all the while sucking blood, sucking, sucking, as in his death throes he blanched and bucked, screamed silently (his vocal chords were destroyed) and died cupfull by cupfull of blood.

Susannah had come in to watch, smiling in satisfaction as Joan killed the man who had so foolishly struck her son.

Tobias thought he saw the shadow of a woman's shape on the stair, but then he heard sounds above him, so Susannah was in her room. He got up, and looked through the door, saw a woman walking down the stairs from the landing. He rushed over, but she was gone. It must be Susannah. 'Susannah?' he called, 'Have you locked the doors? I thought I saw a woman, a woman with Joan's clothes on.'

Susannah appeared above him on the landing. 'We gave them to the workhouse, father, some of them,' she replied, and he seemed mollified, then she added, 'Don't shout again, you'll wake Beamish.'

'I heard you walking about upstairs, thought I heard voices, are you all right? Are you talking to Jarvis?'

'How could I talk to him? He's dead.' She said it matter of factly.

He went up, slowly, looked down on the corpse. No flesh on him, his broken teeth jutting out from a sunken brown and yellow face, his eyes staring, full of terror. His skin was like dried parchment, but he wasn't dry, there was a bluish slime all over him; it smelt of fish, rotten fish. Horrified, Tobias swung round to look at Susannah, who was combing her lovely hair sitting in front of the mirror of her dressing table.

Seeing his expression, Susannah said, 'Enjoy Beamish, your grandson, father of mine.'

Her words were a threat, but they were also a benediction. He turned and went downstairs to get a drink of beer. As he lit his pipe he reflected he would have to get the doctor in again, there was another death in the house.

Hildegard wrote in perfect copperplate as cause of death, *Jaundice. Constitution undermined by intemperance*, pocketed his fee, and went his rounds.

Easter Monday, 1900

Tobias felt young again.

He was walking with his grandson and his daughter. Susannah had her arm in his, and he felt he was a married man out with his wife and son. And they looked a fine pair, he was sure, what with her wonderful looks, flame red hair, and him tall a fine figure of a man. But it had all been hard won. She was a strange woman, a fey woman, revered in Charnegate, Spitalfields, and Whitechapel for the skills that women wanted. Best left alone, he again concluded.

They were in Victoria Park and Beamish walked by his left side, a tall straight boy, with hair so light it was almost white, just like his grandfather's. He had the same large red mouth, with the pendulous lower lip, the same sensual but aquiline nose, the same pastel blue eyes, but his skin was all Susannah's, pale white skin that never browned, only freckled in the summer. (And if people suspected, they said nothing, the women because they needed Susannah, the men because Tobias was hard, and very strong.)

Beamish was a self-contained boy with no friends, but he read a lot, strange books Susannah gave him, books about an old religion, of Babylon, where men paid Temple Hire to go with the priestess at the Ziggurat, and go with her acolytes. And there was nothing Tobias could do to stop him going with his mother to the Crypt. Tobias knew he had him on Susannah's sufferance only.

The years had worn him down. There was his grief still at his wife's death, after that came Justin and Joan's, then Jarvis, all in that damnable Convent. But there was joy in Beamish, and when he admitted it, there was joy from Susannah too. She was so vivacious, had a laugh to make him glad, though sometimes it would make him shudder. She was attentive to him, and made him meals. Her two maids, who were devoted to her, also looked after him well.

It was like being married to his daughter, and there were times, oh passing moments, in the night, when he felt that he *was* married to her, but they were only dreams...

And now he had done the last thing he thought he would have done. Done it last week. She put before him his favourite meal of sirloin steak, cabbage and potatoes, with a thick gravy and a pint of beer. Wearing her most beguiling smile, she said, 'I want you to give me Convent.'

He'd looked up at her in consternation, fearing she meant to leave him, but she said, 'I will always look after you, Papa, and you will watch your grandson grow, but I must have Convent, in my name.'

Or she would leave, she could support herself, in that district, he knew that. 'Then have the damned place.'

Her look of triumph had been fierce. Now, as the sun gleamed on the three of them, Tobias turned to look at her, she was looking up at him, her emerald eyes flashing, her mouth full and succulent. 'What shall you want cooked tonight, Papa?' Beamish looked up at him too, and grasped his hand. Suddenly the years fell from him, and he walked with a brisker step, wondering what tasty treat he'd have, with his daughter's white arms and magical hands preparing it.

He grinned, and knew that he was losing his mind. But that was better than losing them, Beamish and Susannah, because the God he'd prayed to was dead - *they* were alive.

CHAPTER FOURTEEN

Good Friday, Easter, 1906

The sun was falling fast over Whitechapel, the gas lights were being lit by the lamp-lighters with their long poles. Beamish, tall and sixteen, could hear the gas jets hissing on the lamp-posts over his head. He was escorting his mother, his beautiful mother, at whom women smiled. In her basket there were red roses, and some sprigs of hawthorn, with white May blossom.

Once at home, she took him down to the Crypt.

Susannah told him to wait and watch. She strewed the roses on the white cloth, covering an altar, and then strewed the hawthorn. He could see the curved thorns of the roses, and the long black spikes on the hawthorn. Then he saw The Lady, standing by one of the pillars, Her lustrous black hair shining in the lantern light, and her eyes glistened. She wore a red silk robe, though her feet were bare. Around her throat was a gold chain necklace.

Silent, she came to him, blindfolded him with a sash of silk. She led him to the altar, and as he lay down, rose thorns and hawthorns pierced him.

He awoke to find white stuff on his belly. 'Mistletoe,' Susannah whispered, 'mistletoe.' Crushed berries.

The Lady slipped away from him.

Susannah took his blindfold off and led him out of the chamber. He could see, as Susannah lifter her dress to clear the steps in front of him, that her white silk stockings were flecked with red.

Good Friday, 1911

Beamish had just collected a fresh body, a woman the family wanted embalmed, but there was to be no laying in, so no one would be the wiser. He went into the preparation room, stripped to his shirt sleeves and pulled the sheet from the body slowly. Very good condition indeed, he thought, as he put his hands on her thighs. He moved to her head, opened her eye, the left, with a delicate motion of thumb and forefinger. A bright blue eye, the iris only half visible looked back at him. Fresh as a daisy. He closed the eye again.

Her breasts were large, white, milky, firm. The nipples were red, and so were her lips. She had fallen as she was taking a bath, and caught her neck on the taps, snapping the neck bones, breaking the spinal nerve cord, and being paralysed from the neck down, she drowned. Now she was in his care.

Methodically he collected phials, unguents, oils, even a pair of tweezers to depilate her, and began his work. She would get a shampoo and set as part of the labour of love.

His mother had led him into this trade apprenticing him to an undertaker in Limehouse, though she seemed to know a lot about the trade, well the body side of it, instinctively. Oh, he'd rebelled at first, when very young, but only once or twice, since being whipped raw by The Lady, whom he had learned to call Joan or by Susannah was to him less preferable than obeying his mother in everything.

Besides there were compensations: this one was still not cold.

When he finished he went to his office and lit a cheroot, poured himself a quadruple Scotch, sat down and viewed the teeming life of Commercial Street beneath him. It was a good life for him, well known and respected, heaviest drinker, without ever being drunk, in the East End. Could afford it too, from the business, as well as from what Joan got up to, going to the Docks and getting on a ship, servicing the lot of them at a guinea a time.

Easter Sunday, 1911

Joan wore a gown of white silk, with a gold sash around her waist, white silk stocking with red garters, white doeskin shoes of moderate heel, and no lingerie. She was sitting before a mercury-backed mirror set in a gilt frame, in Vestibule. Light from the five large church candles gave her white skin a soft golden hue, it shone on her raven black hair as she combed it. She looked in the mirror. *You are so beautiful. I am so beautiful.*

Joan stopped combing, rested her hands on her lap, staring directly ahead of her, her blue eyes unblinking, steadfast. She did not move her lips. Yes, Mistress?

It's time for Susannah now. She's thirty-nine, and Beamish is twenty-one, it's time for her. We need a man for her. (Joan laughed, low, smutty and vulgar.) *No, not like that, we know she had enough of that. She's taken their seed from them round here. They don't let on for fear of their wives knowing. It will be her father. They don't have to be young, when they love.*

Joan understood her meaning.

She was silent, and began brushing her hair again, reviewing the men she'd used (she could use them in a way that Susannah couldn't, Susannah could only use them as a woman, but her ardency had weakened many of them).

Now Susannah would join her.

Now there would be two.

It was her time, at last, she had waited so long for this. Now she bathed in the bathtub that had once belonged to the mother superior of the Convent, using oil of cloves and lavender water, she felt exultant yet peaceful. Her years of waiting were over, and so much had happened, yet for what was to happen, it was nothing, a passing fancy (young men between her legs, swearing love for ever, older men cynically buying her, there always had to be payment, the mark of respect.

There were blessings, her son Beamish was a great and wondrous blessing; without the Mistress she would never have had the courage to get him on her father, to spring him from her father's loins. Now his time had come, with hers.

She could see her father now, as he was in 1895 with Beamish, five years old, proudly walking him on the wide pavements of Charnegate. Beamish was dressed as was the fashion then, in a little blue frock, complete with frilled knicker leggings and petticoats, his near-white hair long and curled in beautiful ringlets. Yes, her father had been good to Beamish, it was a pity they couldn't trust the old man, but then, he had been too set in his ways to change him, without turning him into a kind of Zombie.

Tobias had spent Easter Sunday reading the newspapers, smoking his pipe, feeding his chickens, glad that Beamish had come over for breakfast with him, even gladder that Susannah made him his dinner - never got used to having maids about the house, but he put up with one now because Susannah insisted (there'd been something about his daughter today, she was quiet and unusually affectionate, putting her hand on his, she even kissed him when she left), now he was preparing for bed.

The trick was to forgot what you didn't want to know. How lucky he was to have a son... no, he only had a grandson. See, the trick was easy, sort of legerdemain.

Like when his brother and Joan died in the fire, just knew it had to be an accident, either that or lose Susannah. And there was the fact he didn't need to work anymore after the fire, because of the insurance, and that meant he could resign his police force job and spend more time with his family, Susannah making wonderful meals, bringing him foaming pints of beer, and Beamish at his feet listening to his tales of derring-do in the police force in the wicked East End.

Who knows, tomorrow, Beamish might play him chess, and Susannah promised him a wonderful dinner, prepared by her white and magical hands... hands of the softest touch, lips of the sweetest kisses, body of the... Daisy, forgive me!

The idea came to him he wanted a bath. Didn't usually bother one month to the next, and he'd had one not two days ago. (But it is Easter.) He frowned, and ran his bath (the maid of course was out, her night off), got out of his corduroys without difficulty, for he was still very strong and very fit, peeled his pullover, (nice Shetland one, Susannah bought him that), his striped shirt, and lastly his vest. Almost forgot about his slippers and socks.

The hot water received him, and he sank back to enjoy it. No need for soap, just soak a while, then dry off.

Later, in his brass double bed, the gas light low, warm in his flannel night-shirt, Tobias lay on his back and thought of Daisy, his wife, who died so long ago, Good Friday, 1872. He could see her by the bed wearing a silk night dress, a red silk nightdress which strained at her breasts and curved lovingly over her hips. She was spreading her long red hair over her white shoulders. Daisy. She smiled, and then slipped into bed with him. Time to make love, then go to sleep.

The dream was so real tonight, so very real (you can still wake up - you know what that means, to wake up, it means to know you are not dreaming).

She was very gentle and very strong, enticing him, it was with shivering delight he entered her. (You know who she is.) He knew now there was another woman in bed with him, one alongside the back of him, and her hands were stroking him, her body against him, making him dazed. (You can't get out now, even if you wanted to.) 'Let me be,' he whispered. But they did not.

They had come into the room singly, first Susannah, and after she was in bed with Tobias, Joan came and slipped in behind him (he had fulfilled himself by then). Their red gowns lay upon the bed like two great wounds.

'You need not worry, Susannah, I will be gentle with him, as gentle as it can be.'

Joan turned him around and embraced him, cradling him in her arms, and legs, then she kissed him, thrusting her tongue down his throat, pulling his manhood into her body (images of slowly sucking out a whelk from its shell, smells of fish, of rotting fruit, of roses, daffodils - he still went to his wife's grave, every Sunday. Susannah insisted). She was so far down his gullet he could not gag, she had a way of letting him breath, so well could she control her tongue.

Soon Susannah was on him too, and then as Tobias began to die, Joan embraced her. As his mind shut down, Tobias felt his daughter change, into something like the dark-haired woman, something rubbery at times, but incredibly strong. He had a vision of a poignard stuck in the base of his skull, pushed up, the blunt blade skewering round, pithing the base of his brain. He died as the women became even more intimate.

Beamish had come in about twenty minutes earlier, and watched his mother and Joan. Tears came to his eyes. It was the end of an era, but also the beginning of a new one. His face brightened, and now there were tears of joy.

Strewth, this was a new one, and no mistake. Now he have two of 'em to contend with.

Tobias, dead, was filmed with an oily bluish slime, his mouth open still where Joan's tongue had been, his manhood shrivelled, his old body looking a decade at least older than it was, brownish and the skin desiccated.

The two beautiful women were putting their silk gowns on.

Overawed, Beamish did not meet their eyes, and they left without speaking to him. He would call Dr Hildegard, and knew he would, like his father, sign the death certificate with consumption, or whatever the current medical fashion was for ignorance.

Tomorrow Susannah would come back into the world for a few hours to tell the neighbours she was going away, America was the place to go. She would attend her father's funeral - one of the finest seen in the district, Beamish would see to that - and then she would ostentatiously leave. But she would be back, in secret.

CHAPTER FIFTEEN

Sam, pushed by Bella out of the lift, floundered into a large candlelit vault, and saw three women before him, tall like Bella. They wore long red silk gowns. Two were brunette, one red-haired, their hair thick and lustrous.

He recognised, fearfully, one of the dark-haired women, she had haunted his memory for so many years. Unless he was hallucinating now, the woman who had despoiled him was right in front of him.

As soon as he saw her, it all came back to him - his rape, of him, by her. The pain, the humiliation, all of it, rushed through his brain like a stinging sludge of hot poison. Flashes of remembrance pierced the sludge, bubbled, formed pictures with sounds and feelings adding to their vile implications.

He'd been kissed so deep he'd vomited. She'd sat on him. She'd reemed him with finger and tongue, the tongue ripping him up as if he were a virgin, blood pouring down his thighs.

There was shame too, when her beautiful mouth drew him of seed, again and again.

...on all fours, ridden.

...on all fours, bidden.

On all fours penetrated so deep, it was an impalement. And all the time, HELPLESS, a woman so beautiful, and so strong, he had been more helpless than a child in her arms, between her legs, under her, over her.

'You!'

Joan smiled, 'Yes, me. Meet my sisters - Susannah, and Josie.'

Sam stuttered, 'That was my mother's name!'

The four women laughed, and Josie came towards him. 'Oh, don't be frightened, we'll take care of you.'

They stood around him, closely. He breathed in their thick, ruttish odour, trembled as they gently caressed him.

'You'll have to do as we say.' It was Susannah speaking, her eyes sparkling, her lips moist, glistening. 'As you begin to understand, you'll see you have no choice. In fact, I was the only one who did have a choice.'

'Choice?' Sam echoed, 'I don't know what you mean.'

'You will.' She turned to Bella, 'You checked if he had any of that acid stuff he made himself ill with last time?'

Bella nodded, saying that he only had medicines now.

'Well, that's kosher.' Susannah concluded, 'We'll make sure Beamish keeps an eye on that. No drug addicts here!' She laughed, and the other women joined in, making Sam even more terrified. He tried to back away, but merely came up against Bella, and when he pushed forward, all four of them enclosed him in a wall of hot breasts.

Susannah watched as Bella, Josie, and Joan, began on Sam, and as she watched, she enjoyed thinking of the past, how she had given birth to Beamish, the joy of motherhood, and her own wonderful passage into a new life. Then came the two schoolgirls into the life of Convent, Bella and Josie, sweet children...

1937

From behind one of the curtained church windows, high in Convent, Susannah watched the children in Charnegate walk to school. But she had eyes only for the girls, in their cotton socks and button-up shoes.

Ten year old blonde Bella said to her friend, dark-haired Josie, 'Always feel spooky when we walk past Convent.'

Josie laughed, 'Don't be daft!' but she felt a shiver down her spine too. And yet there was something calling her from there, promising. She giggled. 'It'll be all right, scaredy-cat!'

Bella and Josie grew from gangly girls to beautiful young women. That Bella was hot-blooded, Susannah knew, seen her teasing the boys, and men, even when she was only fourteen. She was lonely too, had lost her family when a bomb fell in Mode Place, demolishing her house and family.

At sixteen, Bella was, against the odds, still a virgin. She'd been waiting, she felt, for someone worthy of her. She stood five-seven, curvaceous, with such well-developed breasts it was difficult for her to get brassieres. She was very pretty, with long blonde hair, big blue eyes set wide apart in a roundish rather than oval face, and a big cherub bow of a mouth. The local guys said she was better than Betty Grable.

Her time came in the winter of 1943, a late Friday afternoon, as she was coming back from work in the Whitechapel Lyons Tea Shop. She passed Aldgate, then she heard: 'Can you tell me where Convent is, luv?' asked the tall woman with red hair. Fog swirled round them.

Bella smiled, 'I'll take you there. It's on my way home.' She was staying with neighbours.

Outside Convent, Susannah said, 'It was so kind of you to show me the way. Come in for a cup of tea. My uncle lives here.'

Bella hesitated, here eyes wide, the place gave her the creeps, but wasn't she being silly, a cockney girl like her? And anyway, she sometimes liked the place - even if it was an undertaker's - the way the doves cooed and the sparrows so cheerful. The horses too, it was so peaceful there sometimes. She went in with her. Once inside, they had tea in the kitchen.

'But you seem to know the house so well-' Bella said, cutting off her own words.

Susannah smiled, 'And so will you, my poppet.'

Bella would have run, but Beamish came in, pinioned her arms.

'Put her on the table,' said Susannah, 'lie her out, and do her.'

Bella screamed, but to no avail as Beamish laid her out, pulled up her skirt, tore off her panties and - nothing happened.

'Go on, you great lummock!' Susannah screeched, as Joan snickered.

Red faced, Beamish found his spirit willing, but his flesh weak.

'He wants his mam!' Joan chortled.

Susannah was white with fury, told her son to come to her, and out of the corner of her eye Bella watched Susannah do things which soon had Beamish beside himself, excited, wild eyed and - ready.

For the first few days, only Beamish used Bella, watched by Joan and Susannah.

'See how she still fights!'

'Spunky little tyke and no mistake.'

'Look, she's so angry, spitting and swearing!'

'Beamish is going like a goat, he'll tame her.'

Bella gritted her teeth, tried to bear the unspeakable, cursing Beamish Smiley for the animal he had become.

Convent was the base of Beamish's undertaking business, a thriving trade, which he now relished, and worked hard at.

During the early weeks when he had the time of his life with Bella, he often wondered when they'd take his plaything away.

One morning when he was wiping the hearse horses down, Dick and Bess, Gog and Magog (same names, new horses), after two very fine funerals, he guessed that something was up. It was a hot day, and the horses sweated, so he was rubbing them down while they munched their oats. He was a big man with long arms, so the work was not only pleasing to him but he could do it very effectively and quickly. He too was looking forward to his dinner (time was about twelve, and Susannah would call him over to the kitchen in Convent shortly). He wondered what it would be today? He liked boiled beef and carrots, but then, he liked everything she cooked.

He finished up, then started to change the straw, carrying bales as if they were loaves of bread, one in each hand. The sun shone down into the courtyard, warming him.

His heart leapt. Susannah was calling, 'You can leave your work for a while, there's something you should see.'

He followed her into Convent, and down to the first level, vestibule, where they had Bella tied to an altar, ringed by tall flickering candles.

Joan was there too, Susannah said, 'Just watch, Beamish.'

Joan lifted Bella up, pulled her out straight, and then thrust her mouth to hers. Her tongue went into Bella. Bella's eyes turned up in her skull, showing just white. She convulsed, held onto Susannah like a child. Susannah embraced Bella, lay down with her on the cold stone. Already, Bella's body was covered with frothing blue slime. Joan lay, her tongue whiplike, bluish now, engorged, alongside... but her head facing in the opposite direction, her face near Bella's feet. Her tongue retracted, and then slowly, she edged her face to the squirming white hemispheres...

CHAPTER SIXTEEN

As the war years passed into peace, Bella's disappearance faded from memory, but Josie never really forgot her friend. She herself grew tall and attractive, fended off Beamish Smiley's advances - an undertaker, who never got into uniform because his job was protected, like a doctor's, ugh! - kept away from Convent, enjoyed the bustling activity of Spitalfields, and took a variety of jobs in shops, Woolworths was always a great standby, while she and her mother lived in two rooms a block away from Convent.

Smiley's rival came in the shape of short, fat, but attentive and charming, Ben Reese, a tailor, who was doing reasonably well.

The first time he took her out they went to Joe Lyons where Bella used to work, with the white and gold front, big cups of tea, gave her a Player's Navy Cut, with the picture of the bearded sailor on the packet ("It's the tobacco that counts") and talked about his plans for his business with his pal. He painted a very rosy picture. Said he wanted a family. That interested Josie, she was nineteen and unmarried, she was practically middle aged for that area.

It had been a difficult courtship for Ben, she'd blow hot and cold. 'Is that Smiley bothering you?' he asked one Sunday, 'Is that it?'

'He's a perfect gent,' she replied evasively.

Perfect gent indeed! thought Ben. There were stories about that old geezer, but no one could ever pin anything on him. Good client though, thought a lot of himself did Smiley, always dapper, homburg and black suits.

Eventually, Josie said yes, after many maybes. She would marry Ben, time was a fleeting and men were in short supply because of the war.

She was in radiant health, her hair black as soot, her white skin untouched by age, her mouth a rowanberry red, but there was sadness in her dark blue eyes: she yearned for a child.

Josie went to see her doctor several times, and he sent her off to a gynaecologist at the London Hospital, and *he* assured her she was as 'fit a young woman as he'd seen in fifteen years of practice'. The doubt then was on Ben, but he ignored it.

She didn't need a doctor to tell her she could bear a child, every month the tide of life would break out of her, proving her womanhood, and yet at the same time announcing her belly would bear no fruit that moon. At night at certain times of the year, she could see the moon from her bed, in the little flat over Ben's shop in Cripple Way. She watched it arc across the sky with sedate and dignified transit over Christ Church spire. She moved with the moon, but there was no child to cry back upon it, only the drunk by her side who, in his delirium, would reach out with sweaty hands to pluck at her nightdress, to uncover her to more futility. Of late even this pathetic show was failing, and he was becoming impotent. 'It's the booze, luv.' But it wasn't - it was the canker of infertility, and it separated them.

In the May of 1951, her mother died. She had lived with her and Ben for the past few years, and seemed hale enough, but she was always a tense and anxious women, was Peg Nichols, despite her bonny smile and neat bustling figure. She never really got over losing her husband, and being so wrapped up in her daughter, she had never married again. She tightened in on herself, seeing the pain Josie was in, and so Ben found his household divided against him. Sometimes, Peg Nichols would go at him with her tongue, scolding, 'Booze dries up the vigour of a man. Now Josie's father took a drop, but not a bathtub, so work the difference out, Ben Reese!'

He would have thrown her into the street, but knew that Josie would go as well, something he could not abide, for where else would he get so fine looking a wife (and he knew, just knew, that it was he who was infertile). He daren't look at it in the face, buried himself in work, drowned himself in booze.

It was a bright spring day, and perpendicular shadows cut Charnegate up, making her blink against the glare. The tall figure of Beamish Smiley stood outlined in the doorway, his immaculate black suit, black shoes, black tie, and black Homberg, speckless, dustless, shining, too clean.

'Josie, I'm sorry. Accept my condolences.' The words were those of a professional of death, but were tinged with a sincerity which made Josie wince.

'How did you know? It only... she's only just...' She had her hands to her pretty throat. He looked at her red silk blouse from Marks & Spencer, her black cotton skirt, brown nylon stockings and high heels. Then he pushed past her saying, 'You get an instinct after so long.'

She followed him in, he was still talking as he unerringly went to the room Peg sat in. 'I see people in the pub, in the street, and I've seen them for years, and then one day, I know I will be called, for I see a sudden pall about the face, when death has decided to visit.' He put out his hand and with two fingers in a V, closed her eyes with an unhurried deft touch. 'Still warm, it would be better to lay her out now, rather than when she gets stiff, it makes for more dignity.'

'Would you like a cup of tea, Mr Smiley?'

He nodded, and gratefully she went to the kitchen to let him get on with it.

Next day, Josie was mourning and looked a fine daughter in the black car which followed her mother's coffin, dressed in black with Ben at her side.

They were proceeding at a stately pace along Whitechapel Road to Bethnal Green Burial Ground. Beamish could see her face in his driving mirror and he knew she could see him. He let his eyes soften, and saw her stiffen. Strewth! No wonder she did, knowing full well why.

She'd gone round to Smiley's to choose a coffin. He'd been most helpful, pointing out the makes which were dignified yet not too pricey, then he took her to his office to sign the particulars. It was then she first saw the mannequin, dressed in the height of current fashion, standing against a wall, overlooking Smiley's desk. What a thing to see! She gasped in astonishment at so beautiful an object. Such stature, and she no mean height herself; what eyes, and her eyes beautiful too, but not to compare. That red hair! Then she heard Smiley's voice, 'Sign here, Josie, and everything will be fine.'

Josie did as she was bid, and was given a glass of brandy. She was not averse to a tipple, besides she felt at peace near the mannequin, as if those green eyes hypnotised her. She accepted a third drink, and before she knew it, he was standing by her, close to, so when he put his hand to hers to raise her, she did not demur.

The mannequin looked, seemed to look, deep into her eyes, as Smiley lifted her skirt and pulled down her panties, she still had the glass of brandy in her hand. Neither of them looked at one another, but at the mannequin. Once, twice, three times, hard juddering thrusts into her, and then the warmth of seed in her belly.

Perfunctorily, he adjusted his dress, while she bent down and pulled her panties up and smoothed her skirt.

'Thank you, Mr Smiley,' she said, her face flushed, 'I'm sure the coffin will do.' As if nothing had happened.

'My professional expertise at your service,' he replied.

As the funeral cortege left Charnegate, Josie just knew she was pregnant.

Josie would not have a midwife. Ben ranted and raved that she must, but she refused. During Christmas night, 1951, she left him in their bed and went to the bathroom. She squatted down and gave birth just as Susannah had done.

Next morning, Ben found himself a father.

'But... how?'

'It's woman's business, Ben. In the night.'

Sam grew well, Josie would push her pram proudly along Commercial Street, through Spitalfields, passing Convent. From the tower, Susannah would see her, and smile.

CHAPTER SEVENTEEN

Josie was thirty-four in 1961, and her son Sam was ten years old. He smelled her as she thumped around the kitchen in Cripple Way, looking at her swelling breasts in the white BHS gingham blouse, hearing the swish of her gabardine dress that fell like a bell tent showing her fine ankles in flat heeled Clark's shoes. Josie almost never wore stockings except on Sundays when they went to the Methodist Chapter in Commercial Street. Ben never went, he would be over at the Blind Beggar, Brick Lane, talking about the War, and how he won it.

Rabbit, rabbit, and get pissed - that was all Ben was good for these days.

Sam looked at the wild strain in Josie's dark blue sexy eyes, eyes that stared out of an oval pale face. He looked at her full cherry-coloured rosebud mouth.

'Mammy, are we going to have apple pie today?'

'Shush, Sammy, can't you see I'm busy?'

She smiled down at him and he buried his head into her belly She patted him on the head, moved to the gas oven, drew open the door of enamel and steel, peeked inside to see the roast in its tin dish gurgling above the blue pointed flames, set like crocodile teeth beneath. 'Hmm,' she exhaled, 'nice one.'

Suddenly, she grabbed at Sam after she closed the oven door, pulled him like he was just the weight of a doll, and sitting down on the oak kitchen chair by the window, rocked him in her arms on her lap, wanting another child, wanting more than she had.

And she always thought of Beamish. When he saw her, they passed the time of day. He came to Ben for his suits. That was all. But...

Oh God. Now this!

She'd come across drawings, Sam's drawings - of naked women, young girls too. Then she'd realised they were *dead* women, *dead* girls. *Sam must have snuck over to Convent,* and that meant (there were so many drawings) that Beamish knew. Oh God! What was he trying to do?

What was *she* going to do?

Ben came in, Sam went out to play. She hid the drawings under a cushion. Looked up. She didn't like the nervous, *devious*, way he was looking at her. 'You look like the cat that swallowed the goldfish.'

'This needs a drink,' he said, pouring out a tumbler of Haig. 'Celebration.'

She was even more suspicious now, he was crowing - a bad sign. 'Celebration? What for?'

'You know Nunnery?'

Yes, she knew Nunnery, an *avant garde* clothes shop opposite Convent, almost in the market itself. It had a big front window and retail space behind it; upstairs there was a two bedroom flat, and on top of that, a studio, with skylights. Clothes were displayed on two mannequins, a redhead and a blonde one. They were exquisite creatures, each five seven, 36-24-36,(B cup), size five and a half shoes, medium glove size (very long tapering fingers). So ravishingly beautiful were they that often a crowd would stand outside and just look at them. In the past they had worn gold lurex bikinis which revealed every nuance of their beautiful bodies (those long slim thighs, perfect buttocks, deliciously rounded but upright breasts), casual wear (see them in jeans, see heaven) as well as fun party gear. Yes, she'd seen the red-haired mannequin before, but she wasn't going to let on about that, now, was she?

The shop opened Easter 1960 playing rock n' roll with the two mannequins dressed as nuns, white coif, beads, black habit, each adjusting their suspenders, revealing black stockings and red suspenders, *Nunnery!* (Price tags bore the motto, 'Nun Better'.) The nuns caused some outrage, but young people, and not so young, were gearing up for the swinging sixties. Nunnery caught the mood.

The models were dressed by a youngish woman, Joan, who was a brunette, tallish, and very beautiful. But she did not have the unearthly perfection of face that the models had, whose oval faces provided a perfect setting for their wide apart and large eyes (the redhead had green eyes, the blonde blue), the aquiline (yet sensually flared at the nostril) noses, and the wide, generous cupid bow mouths. In profile there was a certain austerity, a purity of line; full on, their faces were compelling, yet softer. Joan was not there often; the shop was run by two girls and an older woman, but it was Joan (so they thought) who did the buying.

Ben went to Nunnery full of expectancy and great curiosity. They had enviously watched the hordes of young people entering it eager to part with their money, while they were still struggling in cramped quarters in Cripple Way.

'A bloody undertaker owns a business like this,' Ben swore under his breath.

Beamish was smiling in a way Ben found offensive, just as he discerned most things about the man offensive, but sensed he might get something out of Beamish.

'I'm so glad you came, Mr Reese,' Beamish hissed, thinking what a stupid halfwit, and no mistake, a toe-rag, and he got Josie! Bloody waste of fine material that. He laughed at his own pun, Reese being a tailor. Anyway, cock, feel her width, and smell her quality. Dismissive as he was of Reese's qualities as a man, Smiley knew him to be a first class tailor, but no businessman. He did quality work for cut prices!

' What do you want, Smiley?'

Beamish sucked on a Gold Flake, and without taking it from his mouth, drawled, 'Been watching you struggle in that little business of yours. Thought I'd do you a favour, on account of I've watched Josie and Sam grow up from babes. Sense of community, got it? Neighbourliness. I think you should expand a bit, have bigger premises, open up a shop for women's gear, they'll buy anything these days, anything for their tight arses. So, I'll lease you Nunnery.' He then mentioned the price, which was so small it made Ben gasp. Smiley caught him before he'd even recovered from his surprise. 'There be special conditions, of course,' he smirked.

'What conditions?'

'You live in the flat with your family, and Bella and Susannah are not to be removed from the display window.'

Ben knew the flat above the shop was better than the one he had already, but on the other hand he didn't like the way Smiley seemed to be ordering him about, so he ducked the issue by talking about the other condition, that of the mannequins. 'Which is which?'

'The redhead is Susannah, the blonde is Bella.'

Bill thought that was no skin off his nose. In fact he'd never seen such great models. But he'd heard Susannah was the geezer's mother's name. Was the guy a nut?

But Smiley went on, 'Your wife, Ben, Josie, will come to Convent and do for me, only twice a week.'

Ben was going to tell him to get stuffed, but the rent! He'd never get a chance like this again. 'Do for you?' he echoed.

Smiley let the moment sink in, then said, with a sudden rush of colour to his cheeks, 'Just about the house, a bit of cleaning, maybe some shopping.' He thought he saw Ben nod, actually nod.

Ben was already thinking of the great window displays he would make with Bella and Susannah. Smiley pushed the lease over for signature. It had been neatly drawn up by Old Jack Regent.

Yes, Josie knew Nunnery, found it... spooky. Those mannequins, they recalled something, *something best forgotten*. 'Well, what about Nunnery, Ben?'

He told her.

Josie's face grew dark, angry splotches appeared on her cheeks, her eyes flashed. She threw the teapot against the wall, and stood screeching, 'You think to sell me? You think to do that?'

'But Josie,' he expostulated, 'we can't turn a chance like this down!' Then with a plaintive, 'It's got a better flat, too. And anyway, what does it matter if you do a bit for him? He only wants to use you twice a week.' Instantly he regretted that turn of phrase.

Josie lit a cigarette, then began picking the pieces of the shattered teapot up, *It all began a long time ago, and it is still happening.* (But what was it that began?) Could she blame Ben? Not really. He was good to Sam even though he looked nothing like him. He'd worked hard, but failed, now Beamish offered him a lease for peanuts, with the rag trade doing well, as the sixties opened up, it seemed young people had all the money in the world and would buy anything. Perhaps he could make a go of it. Perhaps they could, with more space, and more money. It wasn't much of a marriage, but it was all she had. Ben *had* done his best, not everyone could be successful like Smiley. (Bastard!) And she'd better make the best of it, for where could she go?.

She felt powerless, powerless to protect herself, and her son. But surely Beamish would never harm Sam?

She said, listless, 'OK, lets give it a try,' but she was already wondering how she would cope with Smiley now over the road from her, and she going to do for the bastard, the arrogant, smirking sod.

But she had to admit a fascination in him, he was so unlike Ben, Smiley always had plenty of money, always dressed nattily, and was more than respected by the people who lived near, who gave him a kind of deference, and yet at the same time kept their distance. Well, if the sod was up to his old tricks (but he had given her a child when she was desperate, and had never once mentioned what he knew, not even hinted at it) she'd give the geezer a run for his money and no mistake, or she wasn't Peg Nichols' girl.

CHAPTER EIGHTEEN

Good Friday, 1961

Josie got out of the shower feeling refreshed, ready to do battle with Smiley, this being her first day to go over to Convent, even though it was Good Friday.

They'd moved into Nunnery a couple of weeks ago, settled in, and the spaciousness of her new home more than pleased her. She looked at herself in the mirror, noting how nice her skin was as she blow-dried her hair. She'd wear high heels, no stockings, a short skirt, black, and a white cotton blouse, no bra. Best perfume. Had some Chanel. If sex could help her control Smiley, and so protect Sam, she'd use it. No scruples.

She walked determinedly across Commercial Street to Convent.

'What do you want me to do today, Mr Smiley?' she asked, matter of factly, playing it long.

Dressed to kill, he thought, enjoying the look of her. She was a peach and no mistake, with her tallness and well built figure. That little twerp Ben ought to have his stupid head examined, letting her come over like this, into the lion's den. But then losers were all the same, they lost, they did it in different ways, but like as two pennies in that they lost, and then lost some more.

What do I want her to do today? he thought. Well, there was something to get the old grey matter, and the rest, working, wasn't there? Oh yes, she'd find he wanted her to do quite a lot. A fair parcel, you might say.

'You can help me plait some wreaths.'

Smiley was well known for his wreaths and garlands. Josie realised that in Crypt a body would be waiting for Smiley's flowers. She put her hand to her throat in an involuntary gesture.

Smiley's wreath room was part of the stables, it had a glass roof, and it was hot in there when the sun shone. He bought flowers and holly from Spitalfields. Today he had roses as well.

The atmosphere was heady but not unpleasant, for the perfumes of the roses were sweet. The holly gave off a darker more tangy smell. She sat down at the table, took the secateurs and prepared the holly while he braided roses into them after he had fashioned an oval of dark leaves. She watched him work, his hands were very long, the nails well cut, they were a young man's hands, and yet those of an old man. It was something to do with the thinness of the skin, but surely he was an old man, must be in his seventies, but he showed no physical signs. Only in the eyes could you discern his years, they were knowing eyes, they had seen and understood much. His movements were those of a young man, and he was erect even though he was tall. She wondered what secret he possessed, what energy he was plugged in to, to be so vigorous. What were the vibrations, she asked herself, what vibrations does he know and experience? Josie thought a lot about vibrations, she truly was a creature of the sixties.

She smelt a rose, and sighed. She was happy in this room, happy to be doing such beautiful work, work which would help to calm other people's grief. She liked to help people, was always willing. Beamish had said the wreaths were for a woman. Did she have children? she wondered. Children. She was here to protect Sam. Wasn't she?

Beamish said something about it being thirsty work, and went out, returning with two bottles of Cyprus wine and glasses. She accepted his invitation, and they drank, sharing a word or two, smelling the roses, touching the holly.

'Do you miss the horses, Mr Smiley? I remember them when I was a girl. Tall black horses with purple plumes, pulling the hearse all decked out with flowers, and you with your top hat. It was a fine sight.'

'Right enough,' Smiley replied, 'those were the days. More respect then, people had a sense of the rightness of things. Miss 'em like I do my mother. Still, got to keep up with the times, that's why I got the Rollers.'

'What happened to the horses?'

Smiley grinned, 'Sent 'em for a noble retirement, you might say, to live out their lives in a paddock of grass, not a thing to worry their heads about.'

Actually he had shipped them to a French knacker's yard, and they had eneded up part on Parisian tables, and part in dog food, depending on the cut.

He sipped his wine, 'Nectar of the Goddess,' he said. 'I fancies a drop of wine now and then, during the day, when I'm not doing hard work, then it's beer, replaces the sweat, understand, got to do that.' He refilled her glass.

Josie drank fully, relaxing in the sweet atmosphere, and when he touched her breast, she felt at ease, it was pleasant, and it had been a long time since any man had touched her. Why resist? It was like the last time, and that had given her Sam.

Still nothing might have happened, but as she opened her eyes, having shut them in a moment of delicious relaxation, she saw a mannequin, in the corner. A tall red-haired mannequin, like the two in the shop. Like the one she'd seen last time with Smiley, and the effect was the same as before. Those eyes seemed to reassure her, and so as Smiley's hands found her more intimately, it seemed the most natural thing in the world to relax even more and enjoy the wonder of the passing moment.

It was the end of the day, and Ben was fed up. Josie should have got back by now, but he was scared to go over, scared of Smiley.

He wanted another drink, so he poured himself a hefty Haig.

He was going to fix Smiley (he loved his puking dolls), pay him back. Put horns on his head, would he? Josie went out that morning with next to nothing on and she hadn't come home yet, nearly midnight. Pissed him off (wished he could face up to that undertaking bastard, probably knocking her up now on a bleedin' coffin. Sod the pair of 'em). Second pair of horns - Sam wasn't his. He knew that, just by looking at him, but spilt milk? (*Milk*? he smiled.) But good image for a businessman, wife and son. Sound. Put one over on Smiley, and everything would be all right.

He went down into his women's wear show room. For a moment he was nonplussed, the red-haired mannequin wasn't there. What was that sod Smiley playing at, came over and filched the slag? Now here was a chance to get even. Smiley put a lot of store by his mannequins. But then he saw Bella, who by a trick of light, seemed to be staring gimlets into him.

Just you gaze, you little cunt, I'm going to cut you into little pieces, then put you in an incinerator. I'll boil you down to a congealed formless goo. See how you'll like that, you abortion.

Good-looking abortion though. He lifted her leather skirt. Jaysas! Was this mannequin put together! She had a real...

She smiled at him, opened her mouth (was he that pissed?), licked her lips. Her smell rose to his face, of fruit and flowers and rotting fish. He put his hand between her legs, felt her wetness. He brought his hand away, covered in blue slime, but the smell was aphrodisiac. He backed away.

This was just ridiculous! A diabolical liberty of the imagination! He'd dressed the bloody thing not long before, and there was no real... no... just the usual bald mound you always found on mannequins, but, but...

Suddenly, more blue slime oozed out of her mouth, her pores, then she pulled him down to her, her long, hard tongue slid into his mouth with a slick, slurping sound like wet rubber on a window pane.

It was like being sucked out, being... drained, and all the while with a hard on he once would have been glad to have. But not now, as he felt his life ebb away. First a little pulse of death, then a rending pull at him, an agony of feeling, and with the pain, a kind of... love.

When she had finished with him, she took him upstairs. Forced whisky down his throat, then lay him down on his bed, pushed hard on his stomach, then put her hand over his mouth as he vomited. She kept it there until he drowned on his own sick. Drunks do it all the time.

Bella went back to the showroom and took up her position, glinting in the show lights behind the window blinds.

Meanwhile, over the road, Josie moaned, and Beamish panted.

CHAPTER NINETEEN

When Josie eventually went back to Nunnery, she found it closed. She might have stayed away longer, but she had to make sure Sam's clothes were ready - he'd been staying with friends and was due off to school after the Easter holidays.

Ben was not in his cutting room either. Where was he? She searched the flat, and found him in his bed. Distraught, she dialled 999 and asked for an ambulance, the crew of which, on reporting Ben to be dead, called the police.

Later, the coroner was to give a verdict of death by misadventure.

Josie grieved in her own way for Ben, and felt bad that she had been making love with Smiley while her husband had been drinking himself sick. But then, he had drunk himself sick many times before, and the only difference was that this time it had caught up with him. His luck had run out. Many the time was that she had wiped the vomit from his face, and patted his back to make him breathe. Well, all that was over now, and life went on.

She had enough money (all of it blood money, she bitterly noted), insurance money from Ben. Blood money or not, it meant she could send Sam far away from Smiley, to boarding school. She still felt she could handle herself with Smiley, he was a real man, and after years of futile sex with Ben, this was too good to miss. But she certainly didn't want him influencing her son.

By September she had closed the retail business up (Smiley had collected Susannah and Bella long ago. How did he make them? she wondered. And why call one Bella?). She got to see Sam fairly often, he seemed to have settled down at school, and gave every appearance that he would grow up looking like his natural father (damn him), but she spent more and more time at Convent. It was roomy, she liked to cook and it was peaceful; indeed when she was there she always felt peaceful, as if something welcomed her, wanted her.

And there was Smiley, and that meant sex.

Josie awoke lying on a pallet. Above her in the huge vault of Vestibule, chandeliers with was candles glowed and shimmered. She panicked, but found she was unable to move, although she was not bound.

(Why can't I scream?)

Bella, Joan and Susannah came to her pallet. As Joan kissed her, the other two entered her with their tongues. Josie quivered, it was so sweet, so intimate, so *deep*. She felt her body relax, soothing fingers calmed her. Her mind swooned as Bella's tongue delved deeper into her, as the other two did. She saw a lioness in a desert, a beautiful yellow-brown she-beast. It leapt at her, into her brain. She convulsed, as if in sexual climax, then fell back. They delved her with soft slurping sounds (like cats at milk). She felt her sex congeal as Joan left her, then she was whole when Susannah disengaged. When Bella retracted her tongue, her mouth closed over. A momentary spasm of agony as her pelvic girdle shrank to thirty-six.

Beamish picked Sam up at Paddington in his hearse, and from there drove him to Convent. While Smiley had Josie's charred putative body into the hearse in its fine coffin for the burial at Bethnal Green, Sam wept. First his father, now his mother. He pulled himself together. He'd be a credit to her.

After the funeral, Sam had tea (caraway seed cake) with Beamish in the kitchen at Convent.

'One of those terrible accidents, Sam. She didn't suffer though. I don't want to speak ill of the dead, and you know we were very close, but after your *father* died,' (oh yes, he kept that pretence up) 'she found things difficult. Drink, you understand, drinking and smoking in bed.

Sam looked at him with tears in his eyes. 'If only she hadn't sent me away. I still don't understand why I had to go to that school. I bet none of this would have happened if I could have stayed in London.'

'An accident, Sam, that's what you have to hold on to. Things like this happen, going to bed after drinking, smoking in bed...' he let his voice trail away.

'It's like a curse,' Sam observed plaintively, 'all my relatives, *dead*.'

'Yes,' sighed Beamish, 'but it is your work which will carry their lives on, in you. You'll have Ben's skill in cutting, and you know how Josie was thrilled-' the word stuck in his throat, he hoped he wasn't overdoing it, 'thrilled by your drawings.' (She'd never let on.) 'And don't worry about your studio, only the living quarters were badly damaged by the fire. We'll rebuild the flat."

But Sam was still sad, remained so even when Beamish pointed out to him that he was rich, he had a shop and studio. Money in the bank, and of course, the insurance money. Smiley would keep it in trust.

'What about you, Beamish, it was your property.'

And here was the fact that had saved him from investigation by Fire Insurance dicks. 'Oh, it used to be, but I signed over the freehold to your mother several months before the accident, so all the insurance against the property goes to you. Jack Regent's got the papers.'

Yes, the Coroner had done a good job. The police of course had the body forensically examined. The police surgeon estimated age, weight, and build, and it tallied with what everyone knew about Josie. Hardly an arrangement to tax Smiley's ingenuity, used the old Susannah trick, get some indigent slag resembling Josie, and burn her while she was still breathing.

Beamish had had no real anxiety. He knew that there would be inhaled smoke in the woman's body. Charred as it was, he knew it was possible to determine from the presence of smoke chemicals in the lung tissue that the woman had been alive when the fire began. Who could it have been but Josie?

'And I can come here during the holidays - draw the mannequins? Try to dress them?' asked Sam.

'We're counting on it,' Beamish replied.

Good Friday, 1966

Josie lay on her bed looking up with unblinking eyes at the chandeliers and the lighted candles in them above her head. She was dressed in a simple silk gown, and had a necklace of a silver chain, a present from Beamish Smiley. She was Josie, and she wasn't Josie. She was in Vestibule, the second chamber, beneath Crypt, lying with the other mannequins in their beds too.

It was cool in Vestibule, but she did not have the silk sheets over her body. Her hands were at her sides, as if she were laid out, the fingernails narrowing to points, her feet stuck up beneath her gown, and her red varnished toenails looked dark in the candlelight.

Sam would be coming for the day. He was fifteen now. They always knew the date here, one thing they never let up on, dates, so important to them, *Easters*.

Sam came.

Josie looked through at the kneeling figure before her, it was Sam, and he was creating a dress for her (not for her, it was for the mannequin). His fingers were deft. He would make a fine designer. (He did not know she was there.) (If she could cry, she would drop tears upon his head.) He was a tall boy, already over six feet, a fine looking young man.

Imprisoned in the mannequin, Josie was full of motherly pride.

Though this place was terrible, she had found Bella again.

It's not all bad, Josie, mostly it's quiet. You remember when we were little girls together, luv? We used to buy sherbet dabs in Aldgate from Mr Tom's shop on the corner.

It used to tickle my nose. I liked the pop. We played marbles along the gutter in Mode Place. Do you remember your Mam? She was loverly. Don't take on so, luv, you can't do anything about it.

Nor could Sam, as years later, after his desolate time in hospital, he had come back to Charnegate, to be made the plaything of four women, not just one.

CHAPTER TWENTY

Sam had just about recovered from the women's attentions when he first came back into Convent. His medication helped, but together with the terror of being in a woman's power again was his knowing that just as last time, he had not been killed, so he could hope for survival - and be with Mae once more.

So Sam was pliant, complaisant, as the woman played with him, determined not to enter the shrieking pit Joan had forced him into when he'd been a teenager, but soon he realised this was different. True, they had him stripped, were laying him out, first on his belly, then on his back, and were taking liberties with him, but there was no anger, no rage, no real *attack*. It was threatening, they could do what they liked, but though their tongues were out, they did not penetrate him. Like cats with a mouse, they played, they shamed him, but though their talons were out, he felt they were cats who were saving the mouse for another day.

Soon they took to doing their hair, manicuring one another, but Susannah had explained to Sam what he must do, and then he was doing it, in his work alcove, set against the north wall of Vestibule. Everything he needed was there, shears, threads, Singer sewing machines, tapes, all of the highest quality.

Vestibule was huge, very tall, with giant flagstones flooring it. Though the ceiling was vaulted, and there were pillars of some five feet diameter supporting it, you could see end to end from any of the four walls. The south wall had the steel doors of the lift access. In the centre of Vestibule was a stone altar, which he remembered, so it had not been hallucination, it had all happened. The altar was smooth and polished, a pure white marble. Along the west wall, were several rooms, or rather alcoves, open planned, with only partitions, in some cases silk curtains, in others filigreed metal screen, separating alcove from alcove. Each woman had her own alcove, but Sam was puzzled because there were five in all. Who or what was the other one for?

These open planned rooms were hung with silk, furnished individualistically, mostly from Harrods and antique shops, but each had a couch, a table, and a wardrobe. He was astonished to discover that for most of the time these women simply lay on the couches, absolutely immobile, but when one moved, the others usually did as well, as if they were all actuated by the inner spirit. They were very gregarious, often three of them would pile onto one couch, and the fourth would have as well if the couch had been big enough. They did not eat, but they did drink, and their tastes were quite catholic, judging by the extent and variation of the cellar, for a good twenty feet by ten of the east wall was binned for wine bottles.

There were a great number of mirrors, full length mirrors, hand mirrors, and when awake, the four women would spend a lot of time looking at themselves. They combed one another's hair, gave each other manicure and pedicure, massaged one another, and bathed each other (the marble baths were set into the floor with shower cubicles alongside).

Their fingernails unsettled him, they were filed to points, projecting a good half inch from the fingertips. He was put in the mind of a lioness's claws. Idly he wondered if they might come out even longer, even more terrible. If so, they could disembowel with one upward swipe of a graceful arm.

Now he was getting to know them so well, he was disgusted that he had thought they were identical. He, a dressmaker! He had measured them all up.

Dark-haired, blue-eyed Joan was the tallest, but there was only a quarter of an inch in it, he still used inches and feet. Green eyed, redhead Susannah was exactly five feet seven inches. Bella was the shortest, at five feet six and three quarter inches, she had pastel blue eyes. The other dark one, Josie, had extremely black hair, blacker even than Joan, was also blue eyed. She was the biggest built, but again it was a matter of quarter of an inch on the bust and hips, since in effect their measurements were 36 (B-cup)-24-36. They were all long legged, with beautifully shaped shoulders and backs.

The true brunette was called Josie, and that worried him, because his mother's name was Josie. (Don't think about it. DON'T.) And what did Beamish mean when he said his grandmother and mother were there when the four stood round him? (DON'T. JUST DON'T THINK IT.) In any case, he had more than enough to think about. He had to make a wardrobe for the four of them. Expense was no object, Smiley told him that he could spend anything he liked on fabrics, but no, he could not go out and get them, and then there was the matter of the extra dress - who was that for?

Susannah came over, taking her Grecian gown off as she walked, doing it with a grace you might only ever see at the showing in a top dress designer's by - a mannequin. Her hair was worn loosely now she'd undone the golden chain, and she had on Grecian sandals. The other three were sipping wine, titivating themselves. Joan, as usual, looking at herself in mirrors, standing this way and that.

She was standing by him, he could feel her body heat, and he knew that meant she was in a good mood. That saying about people who cut you cold was no doubt true, human beings had something of an ability to radiate or suck energy in. She smelled like oranges, oranges that you have just cut through with a knife, and then pulled apart, ripping the individual vesicles of juice, so it spurted out.

'The party is not far away, how are you getting on with my dress?'

He looked her directly in the face, as he put his shears down, 'It will be ready, Susannah.'

Avidly she looked at the vermilion silk on the table which was taking shape under his gifted hands. 'Do you want to fit me again? I took off my gown for that.'

She liked being touched, and in that was no different from hundreds of women he had fitted, but Susannah did not do it in a passive way; as his hands came in contact with her skin, she would stand taller, and look down at him if he were kneeling, willing him to worship her with his hands. She was so beautiful it was difficult to resist turning on, but now he wanted to get on with his cutting. 'No, let's do that tomorrow.'

Susannah narrowed her eyes, 'Sam, you've *nothing* to worry about.'

Sam got the message. Did as he was told. Her vanity! Got to keep hold on himself, for Mae's sake.

'Nothing to worry about.' Susannah lisped, showing the tip of her pink tongue. Sam had a terrible memory flash of when Joan had despoiled him. Oh Christ! Susannah was getting turned on. Her face was flushed, and a reeking smell of rut and roses assailed him.

Suddenly Josie came over, 'No! For pity's sake, Susannah, you can't have Sam now, go out and get some trade. He's too important to us, he's our dressmaker!'

Susannah compressed her lips, looked a bit shame-faced. 'Strewth, Josie, glad you got me to leave it out. It's just he's so bloody gorgeous!'

Joan was over with them now, and smiled, 'You got that right, he was lovely as a boy, but Josie's right. We don't want to hurt him - unless he plays up.'

They patted Sam, and left him to get on with his work. Shaking though he was, he was determined to out wit these... mannequins.

Mae let herself into Sam's and trudged up the stairs with her suitcase, looking so much forward to their holiday. When she entered the flat, she put her case down, and rushed to kiss Sam, who was reading at the kitchen table, only to find as he stood up and turned round, that she had run straight into the powerful arms of Beamish Smiley.

The shock was manifold. First, the surprise that he was not Sam; second, the latent memory of Smiley ogling her in the street; third, the sudden, always denied, realisation that perhaps, after all, Sam's hallucinations were not hallucinations, but memories, recalled experience of horror.

'So nice to see you,' Smiley laughed and clapped his hand over her mouth. 'Don't struggle, little one, you'll need your bottle and spunk for later.'

With that, he knocked her out, trussed her and put her in a roll of draper's material, a blood red velvet, and easily carried it down the stairs in one arm, while in the other he carried her case.

CHAPTER TWENTY-ONE

Sam noticed that the women were excited about something, they'd come over to him, fondle him, but generally let him be, as they danced together, and drank, kissed, and titivated one another.

He had to finish Susannah's red silk dress for the imminent "party" be ready as soon as possible. He would be able to do it, but only if he worked hard. At least he was being well fed. Within reason, they brought him whatever he asked for, and he suspected that some of the meals were prepared by Susannah. She was a fine cook, but she never said directly she made them, though she was usually absent from Vestibule when the best meals were being prepared.

He had tried to find out if the women had particular weaknesses which he could exploit, but so far had not come up with anything useful. In any case, Beamish Smiley, would prove something of a handful. And there was another thing, he had never hurt anything purposely all his life. At school he'd avoided bullying because of his large size, not through any aggressiveness on his part. If it came to it, just what would he do? It was at that moment he thought of his putative father Ben Reese, little rolly-polly Ben, an unassertive man, not without his East End charm, quiet of temper, but during the war he had been a soldier, even earned a medal or something for gallantry. If Ben could measure up, why, he'd have to. And besides he now felt pretty certain that these women and Smiley had something to do with his family's troubles. Yes, he might be gentle, but there came times when you just had to fight for the good against the bad.

Sam's needle took on a greater tempo, leaving neat zigzags of thread on the silk behind. He frowned with the double concentration of close quality dressmaking sewing and trying to form a plan to escape. His anxiety over Mae was getting worse. He didn't even know if she had turned up at the flat yet, and if she had, what would she do when she found he wasn't there. She'd wait a while... but it was obvious wasn't it, that since he'd been kidnapped, they'd take her too. No, don't think of that. Hope against hope that all is well.

He felt, in this sudden panic attack, for the phials of his medications in his pocket, Piperidyle, Largactile and Mogadon, major tranquilizers which in the appropriate mix stabilised him - otherwise he would be unable to function, but this weakness of his, this dependence, seeded a new idea, perhaps his weakness was his strength?

He forced himself not to take his pills, he might need them for something else.

With cramped guts from worry, he got on with his work, wondering just how long he could keep a hold on himself.

Susannah looked in on Mae, tied to the kitchen table, and gagged. Susannah looked her over, took in her small but voluptuous body, her deep green eyes and auburn hair.

Mae squirmed, to no avail. What in God's name was going on? Where was she, and where was Sam?

Beamish was looking too, and when Susannah came in had been about to molest Mae.

'Leave her be,' Susannah ordered, 'you'll get your share.'

Beamish scowled, 'But why not now?'

'Because it's going to happen with Sam looking on.'

Smiley grinned. Oh yes, he could wait for that.

Susannah gazed intently at her son, realising it wouldn't do to leave him with her, so she told him to go and not to ever be alone with Mae until she said so.

She sat by the fire-grate sipping gin, thinking how well everything had gone, recalling nostalgically earlier days with Beamish, how they had built a haven for them all, and now, soon now, they would be complete, with Mae, five priestesses, just as it had been so long, long ago.

She thought of Sam, and a tickle of desire rustled between her legs. No, she mustn't do that to him, not now, they needed him, not only for the dresses, they had Mae, and that should mean they'd have him, by his own choice, or face a terrible alternative. But her desire was strong. She got up, went to her cubicle in Vestibule and changed. As she did so the other women watched her, and she could tell they too were excited, but everyone had to be careful.

After kissing each of them, she waved goodbye to Sam, 'Just out for a little fun,' she smiled.

Susannah, wearing her red hair in a ponytail, her long legs encased in black jeans, and sporting a purple T-shirt and black leather jacket, stood on her high-heeled red pumps at the door of an all-night burger bar in King's Cross taking in the scene with very hard and very bright eyes. She didn't like what she saw, there was too much misery in the unkempt figures, the dropouts, the broken, but she could feel something else, humiliation, someone had been broken in there, and the wounds were still raw. She detected where it came from, bought herself a coffee, sat down opposite Lili a pretty, long-faced girl, sixteen, with sandy brown hair, made to look wrinkly in a Burns Jones style. She wore black tights, black cotton blouse, black worsted jacket and heavy black mascara, shocking red lipstick, and pink blusher on her cheekbones. She had tiny breasts beneath her blouse (black lace at the throat), a wide waist, narrow hips. She was all of one hundred pounds, and five-two, her fingers were nibbled to the quick. Before her on the composite table was a cold half-consumed cup of coffee, and a three-quarter munched Wimpy burger, with tomato ketchup drooling from its perimeter, like a menstruating oyster. She had a Silk Cut stuck in her mouth, but wasn't sucking in its smoke, which spiralled up, the ash getting longer visibly.

She hunched over her coffee, one ankle over the other under her chair, her head supported by her hands. She was staring into her cup. Tears, at about one every three seconds, it took her that long to squeeze their acidity out of her bleary eyes, fell into the cup on the left side, onto the table to the right. Each tear tracked the same course, a rivulet worn into mascara and make up. She did not sob, it seemed she was just leaking away, a misery so profound, she was dissolving from within.

'Light?' said Susannah, who knew the girl as Lili, one of the homeless young, a prostitute.

Lili did not look up first, then her brain connected with the sound, and she raised her eyes, but not her head. She sat bolt upright, 'Christ, Suzie! Where you been?'

Susannah smiled, 'Business. Give me a light.'

Lili mumbled an apology, and ground her butt into Susannah's Benson and Hedges.

'What's up, Lili?'

In broken sentences, in stifled sobs, but with nothing spared, and with choked shame, Lili's story came out, her words lying flat in air was heavy with cooking oil as the eggs sputtered on the hot plates, the sausages burst, bacon writhed, and burgers browned and sizzled.

After ten minutes Susannah had the full picture. Jess Brown, if that was his real name, probably an alias, had a neat way of getting his kicks. He picked Lili up, took her in his car to his basement flat in the Caledonian Road, north of Kings Cross. Yes, it would be ten quid, just the two of them. He was a big guy, six-two, two hundred pounds, which would be hard meat to earn ten quid on any way. But, but, when they got there, and Lili was lying on the bed naked for him, in walked four other guys. 'You want it baby, well here it is.'

Jess kicked her out in the morning, warning that if she said a dickie-bird, they would do all again, and at the end, slash her face.

Lili knew of other girls who had the same treatment. Not one went to the police, there were no witnesses, it was usually five guys counting Jessie, but once there were eleven.

It was not only mean, but dangerous, Susannah knew, for these girls depended on their sex for money, One day there would be a world where such things could not, COULD NOT, happen any more. One day. One day soon.

'He's out there now, Suzie. If he can't find new stuff, he'll do me again, I know he will. Where shall I go? This is the only place I can get my regulars.'

'How are you off for bread now?'

Lili pointed the thumb of her left hand down. Suzie opened her purse and took out a fresh twenty. 'I got to split now, just scream like hell if you see Jess again.'

Lili looked at the note, then at Susannah, but she was already half way through the door. This time her tears came quick, in gratitude.

Susannah walked out into the night. She knew this Jess by sight, as all street girls know the cops, the regulars, the pubs, and they swapped info, sisters by necessity.

She guessed, and guessed aright, that Jess was not just doing it for kicks, though that was part of it, he would be taking money from the freaks who liked pounding a girl three at a time, watching her squirm. There were many guys who didn't have the bottle to pick up a whore, and even then had to get their rocks off as part of a wolf pack. She felt hungry enough for - how many was the highest score Lili said - eleven? She'd settle for five, including Jess.

Susannah saw Jess's Ford Granada (done up in two-tone, blue and black) on the ramp at Euston carpark across the road. All she had to do was wait for him to come down.

'Why lookie, here,' he said, catching sight of Susannah. (Just one more lonely cunt, waiting, wanting, to be filled. Jess knew that about whores, that they were wanting, and waiting, and though they said they were in it for the money, take away what they did, and there was no life in them at all.) 'You like a drink, luv?' To his surprise, for she had declined him in the past, Susannah nodded. He was thinking there was going to be a lot of fun for him and the boys tonight. Susannah was a peach, tall and stacked (wonder how long she goes before she begs?).

He took her arm, liking the perfume of her and the flashing teeth in the sodium lamps. He took her to a pub that had barely altered since Victorian times, nestling behind St Pancras.

Jess drank Heinneken lager from the can, chased it with Teachers. Susannah had vodka and lime which she sipped but did not finish. The pub was mostly full of regulars, though here and there tourists huddled, wishing they had not come into this particular London pub because the local colour was a bit, well, too local and too colourful. Porters, train drivers, post men from the British Rail wagon sorting offices, cleaners, earnestly knocked back their drinks, amidst a loud buzz of conversation. On the colour TV they were showing a re-run of Liverpool against Arsenal, it was that kind of night.

Jess was about thirty-five, tall and meaty, dressed in young man's baggy suit, shoulder pads, thin black tie, white boutique shirt, Church's shoes. The gold chain around his left wrist was inscribed in copperplate writing, "Jess". He had a face like Barry Manilow, but more elongated, with a bigger chin and narrowly set brown bleary eyes. He was also dark rather than fair, his greasy hair glinted in the bar lights (spots from Habitat, 100 watt bulbs, the landlord's only concession to the twentieth century). He smoked St Moritz and exuded a liberal smell of Brut. He was, thought Susannah, a prick.

He didn't need a line of chat, with her, did he? You know what I mean? Her being a brass, an' all. So he just sat and got fighting fit drunk. Then he put his hand on her knee, told her he was making a few phone calls, 'Cos were going back to my drum, girl.' Susannah smiled, it promised to be quite a night, he was setting her up and telling his pals to come in. *Something real tasty tonight, lads, a bit of upper drawer.*

'Jess,' she smiled, 'why not come back with me? I've got a few friends.'

She watched suspicion turn to interest and caught the jolt of lust in his eyes. She was offering him a bleedin' harem!

He roughly, momentarily, groped her, wondering vaguely that something didn't feel quite right. But she had her hand on him, so he didn't bother. Cool customer, he observed, and laughed.

'OK. Let's go.'

She put her hand on his knee, 'Just you wait a minute, I've got to take a pee. See you outside.'

Jess finished his drink, then went out, saw Susannah up the street towards the gas works, now an industrial monument, where the orange sodium lights were getting progressively less. She smiled, and beckoned him to her, suggestively touching her crouch. Thinking that she was probably going to give him a blow job, or a knee tremble in one of the alleys, as a sort of starter to the evening, he went up to her as she disappeared into a cul-de-sac.

Yep, there she was, skirt up.

He went in on her, forcing her down to his crotch, but couldn't believe he was unable to make her, and was even more surprised when she stuck her mouth against his, and her tongue broke through his teeth, tore out his tongue, as she held him inescapably close.

He writhed, gurgled, but could not break free, as the agony inside his head increased, until with a peak of pain she retracted her tongue and he fell to his knees, blood pouring from his mouth.

Susannah smiled, then taking him by the hair, smashed his face to a pulp against the wall.

Just another corpse from a gangland killing. These pimps were doing it all the time.

Quickly and efficiently, Susannah went through his pockets, and found well over four hundred pounds. Never give it for free.

No one noticed the girl with the head scarf in the shadows waiting her time to come back into Kings Cross. She walked fast, feeling blood soak into her, and knew it would be some time before the gore on her clothes would disappear too, absorbed, fresh blood with its energy giving properties. It was coolish under the railway arches, but dark. Apart from a few drunks, the zip-zip of passing cars was the only life.

One car slowed down, kerb crawling her. A guy with a thin moustache and a bald head on the passenger side rolled down the window of the Audi, 'Hello darlin', want to give us a good time? We got loadsa money.' He seemed to find that funny, and turned chuckling to his driver companion. She looked at them, and smiled, 'Not tonight, got the rags up.' That took the smile away, washed it clean off like a Kleenex takes snot from a child's face. The car accelerated away with driver's imprecation, 'Filthy slag!'

Time to catch a cab for Charnegate. She felt the sleeve of her leather jacket which had caught some blood spray, it was clean. She sighed with relief.

She stood on the wide pavement, hailed the first cab she saw. It came over and to her surprise, a woman was driving. There'd been a few, she'd heard, but this was the first time she had ridden with one. Tough cookie, she thought. The woman, youngish, and cockney blonde, grimaced when she heard the destination. 'That's all I need, won't get a fare back,' she grumbled.

'Don't worry love, said Susannah as she settled herself back, 'I'll give you a good tip. Plenty where that came from.' And she laughed, remembering the look of astonishment and terror, but above all pain, in Jess's eyes.

When she got back to convent she went straight in to see Mae, who had by this time stopped moaning, though still gagged and tied to the kitchen table. She'd begun to take stock, really take stock, of her situation. She had bitten down her panic, now she had to think.

They wanted her alive, that was obvious, they'd tied her, but with silk scarves, so her circulation was flowing freely. It meant she had time, she didn't know how much, but any was a godsend.

Beamish Smiley - she'd seen the lust in his eyes but he hadn't really dared to use her, he was scared of that red-haired woman. Why would so powerful a man be frightened of her?

Then Susannah was over her, looking down at her, smiling, saying, 'It won't be long now, little one.' She bent down to kiss her forehead.

Mae of course could not avoid her, but she tensed. Then to her surprise, as those beautiful lips came into contact, she felt a wonderful pulse of pure restfulness pass through her, and she was no longer afraid.

Susannah unwrapped the gag from her mouth, and kissed her. Mae, despite herself breathed in the heady smell coming from Susannah, roses, wine, and a deeper odour, musky and fragrant like no perfume had ever been.

Mae gazed into Susannah's beautiful green eyes, and again felt at peace. As Susannah lifted her head, Mae said, 'Untie me, let me go. Where is Sam?' Questions bubbling out of her.

Susannah smiled, 'Never mind now, my little duck, you have nothing to worry about, so don't worry. Everything will be all right, you'll see.'

'Then let me go.'

She watched the woman's eyes harden, now like agate, 'Try to be your age. Why would we get you, only to let you go? You have to understand new things, Mae. Be like me.'

With that, Susannah put the gag back on, and left her, leaving behind a smell of fish, and roses.

CHAPTER TWENTY-TWO

The morning of the evening of the party.

Beamish watched Sam putting the finishing touches to Susannah's vermilion silk dress. He was across Vestibule from him, saw his needle flash as he stitched beneath the fluorescent light.

Wonder what he'll say when he finds out Mae is here? He stole a glance at Susannah, she blinked, her green eyes hard. She's looking forward to trying her dress on, she always did like a bit of show.

Beamish checked out the fifth cubicle, seeing for the tenth time all was well. The couch came from Christie's, cost him thirteen hundred pounds, a *chaise-longue*, very early nineteenth century. Her tiny chandelier was Venetian, twenty candles. He grimaced, that was a pain, keeping the supply of candles in their holders, but the light was beautiful and soothed the girls, harsh electric light tended to make them a little fractious.

Sam looked up from his stitching (the thread was gold) watched Beamish pulling then patting at the silk sheets on the couch in the fifth cubicle. It dawned on him that the arrival of whoever this cubicle was for might very well be imminent. There was a slight anticipation, an air of expectancy about Beamish this morning.

Sam told himself to keep control, keep stumpf too except when he was trying to find something out. And there was something else, something Beamish said, about never needing to worry about getting old. Well, he had never really given it a thought, after all it was natural, and he didn't like to interfere with mother nature.

The size of Vestibule was so great that there was no actual feeling of being incarcerated, no claustrophobia, in fact there was a sense of space. Sometimes though, he would

117

get a whiff of rotting fish, or squashed and mouldering oranges, reminiscent of Billingsgate Fish market and Spitalfields respectively, it was sharp enough to be disturbing, and it usually happened when one of them was going to the shower. (They parted their lips to show their perfect teeth, their pink tongues, energising in the flowing water.)

In any case, he was used to being confined; there had been times in hospital when he was in a straitjacket in a small padded room, with no one heeding his cries. Whereas here, he thought if he cried, they would console him (more than consolation was now promised) no harm would come to him as long as he did not bring it upon himself (So you tell yourself, but have you wondered what they want from you? Just to make their clothes? No, you can't be that naive. Not so naive, when you think queens had their own dressmakers) And after that?

Stitch and be merry, for tomorrow we may die.

And that we may die, is always true.

He could feel her warmth, he did not hear her come over to him but he could feel her gentle warmth on his face. He looked up from his work, Susannah stood by his side, her feet on the Axminster red carpet, her wondrous nakedness close to him. She smelt of jasmine, and the sea. 'Nearly finished, Sam?' she asked, her voice sibilant, reassuring.

'Finished, Susannah.'

He got up and put the dress on her, a simple Grecian style, off one shoulder, almost revealing her left breast. It seemed seamless, so expert was his stitching, curved over her abdomen, over her hips, was snug and lithe on her thighs and buttocks, down to her knees. He picked up her shoes, the ones she'd worn to fit the dress, bent down, slicked them on her feet, then they walked over to the huge gilt framed mirror at the end of his workshop. She regarded her image, and smiled. 'You've done well, Sam, it's so good, better than Dior, or Yves St Laurent.'

'You can wear white silk self-support stockings with that dress,' he said, marvelling as much at her perfection as his own ability to get her so well moulded by his dress, 'but underwear, no, spoil the line.'

Susannah laughed, and as she did so, lust for Sam again overcame her, Sam backing away as he recognised the signs, tongue lisping between her lips, her indescribable smell, so powerful, so ruttish, fearing as he did, being impaled.

Quickly the others came round, and Sam feared the worse, but it was Susannah this time who rose above the situation, 'Let's have some rough trade, and let one of us bring back something for Sam to see, before the festivities, so he never gets any wrong ideas.'

Beamish was looking on anxiously, but clearly had the sense not to interfere.

The women spoke to one another agitatedly, and the smell of their excitement and what they could do nearly suffocated Sam.

He got the gist of it though, they were going out on a kind of last fling before IT - whatever that was, but which involved him - happened.

Suddenly, they all went to their respective cubicles and dressed to go out into the teeming streets of London.

Susannah came out from Convent's side gate wearing a brown suede skin jacket (that set her back five hundred quid), F.U. blue jeans, a white cotton T-shirt, red high-heeled shoes. She had nothing else on, but over her shoulder was a black leather bag, from Liberty's. She wore her red hair in a ponytail. It was already dark, but the streets were busy and she always scanned before she opened the side gate.

She would walk east to Whitechapel, then catch a bus to High Holborn, then the tube to Hyde Park, then cab to the London Hilton.

Her loins were tingly, soft as petals. She was hungry for men, but girls would do.

Joan walked along Mount Street, Mayfair, her miniskirt revealing shapely legs in black net stockings. Her handbag was large and shiny, wet leather look; her blouse was finished with a cravat - and her donkey jacket, a splendid canary yellow, tied with a belt. She wore a black beret. She had been there only a few minutes after getting out of the cab, but she was kerb- crawled by a Porsche almost immediately.

The guy who spoke to her, Charles Darbay, was in his forties, a large red-haired man in a Savile Row suit, wore a white shirt and a red tie. He had a military moustache the size of small brush, hair brushed back off his forehead, and a a pink well-scrubbed face. He didn't ask the price, just said, 'Getting in?'

As if she'd known him all her life, she walked round the car, and got in. As they chatted inconsequentially, she nodded in response to his pertinent question, 'Back to my flat?'

Joan guessed he must be at least sixteen stones.

Half an hour later, she was kneeling nude before him in his Jermyn Street flat. He moaned with pleasure as he climaxed. 'Oh,' he cried, 'you are so wonderful, a goddess! He entered her with great delicacy and consideration, just as he had read in *Cosmopolitan*, couldn't believe the pleasure she gave him (her eyes are liked those of a tigress. She smells of...)

He was suddenly afraid, but he was ever more quickly drained of energy, and fell into a coma in her arms.

She stayed with him for another ten minutes, by which time the pink glow to his face had changed to a deathly pallor, and the healthy colour of his body was transmuted to a lardy white from which black hairs tufted in permanent goose-pimples.

Joan let herself out after taking her hire from his wallet - one hundred and fifty pounds in ten pound notes.

When Darbay woke up at about twelve, he had fond memories of the lovely woman he had paid for. But he felt so cold. With great effort, shaking like a dog just out of water, he sat up and swung his legs over the side of the bed. With mounting horror he looked down at his thighs: they were those of an old man, the skin crinkled, the flesh raddled, the muscles wasted. Still shaking he tottered to the bathroom, looked at himself in the full-length mirror. He was emaciated.

He began to sob and scream.

The porter heard him and crashed into the room. He took one look at Captain Darbay and dialled 999. The ambulance arrived promptly, carried him to St Mary's, in Paddington, where over some months he was tested for cancer, and everything else they could think of, but he continued to waste away, and eventually died.

The London Hilton, Hyde Park Corner, the same evening.

Susannah smiled at the doorman who was holding the cab door open for her as she gracefully slid out. She gave the cabbie ten pounds, and waited for her change, she did not tip, went into the coffee shop. Within five minutes, a Saudi Arabian guy was chatting her up. As it happened, his suite was in the Dorchester, he'd come over to meet a friend, seen him, and then he saw her.

Ben Saud was tall and thin, in impeccable English suit, but rather odd cloth, a wide check, brown and darker brown, silk shirt, silk crimson tie. He spoke without an accent, and gave off perfume, a woman's perfume. His black hair was parted in the English manner, and he was even handsome. Bella guessed he was about thirty, rich and influential. Healthy too.

Saud served her with champagne and caviar, then stripped her himself.

He lay her on the bed and tongued her private parts. His mind reeled with the scented pleasure of her. Her secretions were like a drug, he thought. Frenzied with desire, he entered her, deliriously speaking Arabic. She thought she knew some of the words, a memory trace of long, long ago.

She held him with herself internally, until it became painful for him.

He last remembered her smiling as he plummeted into unconsciousness.

She took over three hundred pounds from his briefcase.

Later.

Bella sipped white wine in the Cumberland Hotel. She'd only been there a few minutes when a young guy struck up conversation with her, he had no idea she was whoring. Said he was a poet, had an infectious laugh, was dark-haired, quite good looking. She sensed he was shy, so she suggested, 'Why don't you read me some of your poems, in your room?' He was thunderstruck, complied eagerly. Bella seduced him easily, both of them were soon naked.

'You are so beautiful,' he said, falling on his knees before her, 'let me worship you with my body.' She let him. After he became comatose, she took his money.

He awoke later feeling fatigued, and drained.

At about the same time as Bella worked the young poet, Susannah's trick, Saud, was shivering, looking in utter disbelief at the black strands on his white dressing gown. His hair was falling out in tufts, leaving his scalp raw. He brushed at his head with his hand, it seemed that his scalp slid, like a fried egg in a non-stick frying pan, slid like a greased toupee, and came away in his hand. With an effort of will, he dialled his embassy.

While he waited he went back to the lavatory to micturate, but as he fumbled to relieve himself he realised with horror that there was nothing between his legs but a sort of crinkled, nosed, pouch, just skin.

He flopped against the cold tiles of the bathroom wall, and feeling his strength desert him, slowly slid down. The embassy aide found him weeping.

Shortly thereafter, Saud was flown back to Saudi Arabia and installed in one of the most up to date hospitals in the world, built by British personnel, manned by Europeans and Americans, where he was treated for radiation sickness, and cancer, and AIDS. He was to live another few months, and kept babbling about a woman who had infected him, so he said, but no one could really make head or tail of it. Eventually, despite all that was available of western medicine in this private kingdom, Saud wasted away, and died, hardly six months after his fateful meeting with Susannah.

Leicester Square.

Josie got picked up by three very large and boisterous German tourists, boys of eighteen coming on nineteen. She seemed very young - jeans, Puma trainers, pullover, ponytail, duffle bag. They had a few beers in the Porcupine Pub, Cambridge Circus, and discussed how they might get her into their rooms at the YMCA. Eventually she suggested they book in at an hotel. No way, they complained, couldn't afford it. She astounded them by saying she'd see to the room, but they still had to pay a fee. She saw how excited they were. Might they well be, she would show them how all three could have her at the same time.

An hour later, there were three naked German youths in a Strand Palace bedroom, lying in a tangled heap upon a bed. Their teeth were chattering with cold, though the room was warm.

By morning some of their vigour would return, and though they never fully recovered their youthful energy, they did not die. They barely had the strength of seventy year olds, they even moved like old men, and back in Germany were prized specimens for doctors to study, as examples of some kind of auto-immune dysfunction - though no one could say what.

Night was falling, and Joan had done a few Johns in alleyways, they thinking they had landed in seventh heaven as she serviced them, only to find when they got home that they were less than they had started out, a curious kind of atrophy of intimate parts.

In a sense, Joan had been saving herself, and in the event, she found her mark at Kings Cross, gave him that look every man in the world recognises. She walked away, knew he was following her. With legs like hers and the face she had, what else could the poor fool do?

Derek Smith was newly divorced, emotionally vulnerable (apparently men suffer more from divorce than women, especially if they don't have a new partner, something to do with them not being able to drive a washing machine, the accumulation of dirty laundry saps the spirit - that and having to get their own breakfast). He was of middling height, wore a decent Burton blue serge suit, his hair was fashionably long, but not hippy length. He had a face you see a thousand times a day in London, pinkish, with features that were entirely unmemorable. His shoes were brown, Marks & Spencer.

He could not believe his luck, the woman was so beautiful she took his breath away.

She was easy to talk to, and within minutes he was bubbling over, telling her everything about himself. He still couldn't believe his luck, and even said, 'What's a nice girl like you doing this for?'

'I do it for love, and money,' Joan replied. 'We'll stretch our legs,' she said.

She got him to Convent by back alleys, by walking in shadows.

The blow caught him totally unawares. Only the heel of her palm into his forehead, but it connected with a sickening thud, jerking his head back. They were sitting at Smiley's kitchen table, drinking Scotch, and she just suddenly threw one at him. He saw it coming for a split second, and thought: *This can't be happening.* Then he fell off the chair, unconscious.

Joan smiled, lifted him up, carried him like a child, hobbling a little on her high heels, pressed the button for the lift in the hall and as the steel doors hissed open, she dragged her victim in. She pressed the requisite button, the lift went down forty-five feet to Vestibule.

Sam had been working furiously on some tiny last minute changes as Susannah, Josie, and Bella, laughed about the day's fun, and drank copiously, fawning on one another, and coming over to him form time to time to give him a kiss and a fondle.

Suddenly the lift doors hissed open, and Joan came out dragging her prey with her, her eyes vibrant with bloodlust.

Sam was mesmerised as the women fell upon Derek, stripping him, their tongues darting out, sweat pouring out of them with excitement, as they stripped one another, and set to.

Sam got up to help him, but Beamish, who had now arrived, pushed him back on his stool. 'There's nothing you can do, nor for that matter I can't do a tinker either. In this mood, they'd tear you apart. Besides, look upon it as an education, of what might happen if you cross us. In a way, the show is for you, sort of an educational experience.'

When Derek came to, he felt warm and snug, could smell the sweaty perfume of a woman making love to him. She was laying belly to belly with him, but they were on their sides. She had one leg crooked over his thighs, and she was pressed tight against his chest. He was aware that another woman was laying up against his haunches, but her body, though warm, was not moving. It was Joan.

He could smell fresh flowers, and the stench of fish. But he didn't care. He had never done anything so naughty before, and was about to get stuck in, when he recalled he'd been slugged out. That realisation, and the fact he could see a tall man looking at him with a malignant sneer upon his face, made him panic, and struggle.

'Go on, Bella,' Smiley said, 'get stuck in!' As if she needed any encouragement.

The pain started sweetly, like being tickled with a fingernail that cuts deeper and deeper. Except that fingernails were somehow inside the woman he was inside of.

She was sucking at him, inside her, sucking at him with herself, and now she put her tongue into his mouth, smashing his teeth. He convulsed as her tongue went into his hard pallet, as if searching for his brain.

Sam struggled past Beamish as the women had their fill, only to be struck down with a savage blow to the head. He watched from the floor, having been unable to get up. At one time the women had allowed Derek to run around as they stalked him, he whimpering and bleeding, only to be caught, and impaled, the tongues coming out of him rust red with blood. Then they spread-eagled him on his stomach, and it was Bella who took him, from behind, her tongue penetrating deeper and deeper, until with a plop it poked out of Derek's mouth.

The man was still alive, just, but had little left to give. Bella took a little more, then drew back to let Joan have her turn. When she finished, it seemed he had been sucked dry.

Beamish dragged him out contemptuously by the ankles as he whimpered in death throes. 'You piece of garbage, even a coffin's too good for you.' He took him to the lowest chamber and threw him head first into the Pit. Even as the writhing body hurtled into the blackness, Beamish heard the patter of rats as they scurried for their meal.

Susannah came up to Sam, her beautiful body wet with sweat and streaked with gore. 'You've just seen what can happen, cock sparrow. So just you mind your manners.' She tucked him under the chin, saying as she turned away, 'Strewth, I could use a drink.'

Shaking with shock, Sam watched them drink, hug one another, and laugh. As he gradually took control of himself, hating them, hating and hating, he saw the rust marks of blood on them gradually disappear, absorbed by their skin.

Then they showered and lay on their pallets, making Sam think of some kind of serpent which sated, must sleep.

CHAPTER TWENTY-THREE

Smiley checked the tables for the evening's festivities, hoping that Josie would take an even greater interest, as she was more attuned to the nineteen nineties than Susannah, who tended to make a place look late Victorian.

He rearranged the three dozen roses in their three vases, moving with deft assurance, inspecting the silver service, the wines, folded the napkins again. He would lay the cutlery soon, set places for two men, and five women.

He was about to leave Vestibule when he caught sight of himself in one of the mirrors. There was a something on his face, a crack, running from his mouth, at the corner, to his eye, straight across his nose, and it was seeping red, baring the bone beneath. His lips too had shrunk, like those of an old man.

He cried out for Susannah, coughing, hardly able to move, she heard him, and came downstairs by the lift. He fell into her arms.

Sam looked up, and stifled a cry. Instead of the tall and strongly erect figure of Beamish Smiley there was a scarecrow of a man, with a livid gash on his face, his body emaciated, his clothes flappy upon him, bald headed, scabby with liver spots.

Sam had looked up from his work, instinctively had risen to help, then realised the last person in the world he could help was this monster, this sod, his father, who had got him into all this. Still, it was hard for him not to help, against his very nature. He forced himself still, then watched as Susannah kissed the wreck better.

Minutes later, with Sam having been told by Susannah to get on with his work, and stop gawping, Smiley was in his office, where he lit his usual cheroot and liberally served himself scotch, as was his wont when things got trying.

Now he was himself again, a man in his prime, he congratulated himself, noting with pleasure not only his reformed body, but the excellent cut of his suit - one of Ben Reese's - and was glad, he thought, to have got so many out of the little toe-rag before they finished him off.

His appearance was still startling to people born thirty years after him, who were shrivelled and bent, though there were hardly any left. Those who had not died, moved out to more salubrious climes, mostly Stamford and Golders Green. As the Jews, cockneys, and Italians moved out, so the Bengalis, Pakistanis and Punjabis moved in. They spelt safety. They didn't know who he was, and didn't care. The Moslems built a huge copper-domed mosque in Whitechapel and the developers were going to gentrify Spitalfields. The market was going to be destroyed. He'd seen what they'd done to Covent Garden, and didn't relish the change.

There was nothing in him but wonder and joy that he had such vigour and health for so long. He'd been a man in his prime ever since his prime, a half century with increasing powers, without illness, while those of his real age had already succumbed. What was the latest insult of old age? Alzheimer's disease, they turned into vegetables, shitting and pissing, not even knowing they were there. Stuff that for a game of soldiers. NO MATTER WHAT HAPPENS NOW IT HAS ALL BEEN WORTH IT.

He got up, tall and elegant, poured himself more Bells then sat down and drew on his cheroot, sampled the Scotch. He was as snapping fresh now as he'd been fifty years before. Pius the Pope had lamb embryo cells squirted into his buttocks, so did Somerset Maugham, and what did it do? Kept the body in its seventies, a decade younger, but the mind still turned to squirming worms. His mind was sharp.

This country had millions of farting old people, he gloated, who hadn't even got all their marbles, sitting about in hospitals and rest homes, He suspected that a lot of violence was caused by young people simply because they had seen a gaggle of the aged being driven around in an ambulance, and it had scared them shitless.

Besides, in the pitifully short period of real vigour average human beings are given, there is no time to do much. If you had a half century of vital maturity, you could experience a great deal. He had just begun to learn to play the organ, a wonderful thing, Yamaha. He'd always envied those sods in the churches where he delivered and collected the coffins, playing requiem masses. Now he could belt out a bit of Bach with the rest. A touch of *Land of Hope and Glory*. Wonderful sound. Ordinarily he'd be stone deaf and arthritic by now, if alive at all.

And there were the inexhaustible wonders of sex.

If only Sam could really grasp the opportunity!

As for Mae, she would learn so much, so quickly, so soon.

He laughed and rubbed his hands together. Could scarcely wait.

CHAPTER TWENTY-FOUR

It was coming up to midnight, Sam sat opposite Beamish at the wine table playing chess. He'd often wondered how condemned men could play cards with their guards, only hours from execution. Now he knew. In the background Chris de Burgh was singing *Lady in Red* (they'd previously had Bonnie Tyler). The game was slow because both men were drunk on Claret, topped up by tumblers of Haig. Alongside them, the four women were lying on their backs staring at the fluted flames of the candles in the chandeliers.

'You can never gauge their mood until it happens. Take the other night, a lot of guys got theirs. Good thing they only do it when they are hungry, but you can never tell when that is - except they go out, but there's no warning sign.'

'You mean,' Sam gasped, 'they go **out** and do what they did to that guy and to me?'

'Worse,' Beamish replied, drawing on his cigar. 'I can tell you, it worries me sick sometimes. I mean they leave wrecks behind them. You wouldn't credit it. But London is so big, there's no way anyone can see a pattern in it. I mean one guy here with his pecker off, another drooling like an old fart, no agency to cohere it, to see it. Also, they are usually very discreet. It's just that tonight is the night, and they wanted to be really charged up for it. You'll see what I mean soon.'

Sam tried to get more information, but Beamish fell silent, concentrating on the chess game, a real chess freak, him. Sam grunted, watching Beamish take his queen's white bishop. He was not really concentrating on the chess, he was thinking about getting out, and he was worried sick now about Mae. What would she be doing now? Gone to the cops?

'Check and mate!' Beamish crowed.

Sam looked, and saw that it was. Not that he cared, he'd only played to see if he could get something out of Smiley.

'It's all very well to talk about the fun you've had, but when you get down to it-' Sam was controlled, but there was no doubting his determination to beard Smiley, as was shown by the set of his mouth, '-when you really get down to it, your enjoyment is based on cruelty. This ghost, this ghoul, that Susannah and the rest talk about, if she exists at all, must be one of the meanest minded slags the world has ever come across.'

'So would you be if you'd been through what she has. But be careful what you say, she's very touchy,' Smiley replied. 'Besides, all what you say just boils down to a sickly gob of sentimentality. What in hell do you think life is but hating and hurting.'

'Love and caring, you old fart but I guess that is beyond you.' Sam replied, hotly.

Smiley laughed, 'Bullshit, me old cock sparrow. You have to take your good times when you can. And for you, that is going to be sooner than you think.'

Sam was not mollified, but felt helpless against Smiley's assurance, his arrogant certainty that he'd done the most sensible thing, no matter who else had to pay.

'Got it all worked out, son?' Beamish mocked. 'You've got it made, if you only knew. Just think, you'll never be poor, the Mistress is extremely able where money is concerned. You'll never have a day's sickness, and you'll end up living at least twice your natural span, fit and young. Also,' he chuckled, 'who else gets to be able to park his women in a clothes cupboard, and leave them for weeks on end, and when you come back, they are as good as new?' He warmed to his subject, 'Men have always fantasised about sex slaves, about women as pliable dolls, things you can put away and take up again, I guess they're the result of that yearning, a global wish-fulfilment. And like the man said, be careful when you get what you really want.'

Sam furrowed his brow, 'Sex dolls? Pull the other one, Smiley. These women aren't anyone's sex fantasies, they destroy people, you said so yourself. Hardly pliable, I'd say.'

Smiley laughed, 'Well, I can understand your jaundiced view, considering your experiences with them, but they will let you do anything you like, any how you like, if they trust you. Me, I'm the luckiest guy in the world, sex fantasy in reality.'

And you are their slave, thought Sam.

But Smiley wasn't finished, 'Come on Sam, be fair, aren't they the most beautiful women in the world?'

Sam pounced, 'Can they have children?' He had a vision of incredibly strong little titans, or would there only be females? He wanted children by Mae - real children.

Beamish shook his head, 'No, it would be unnecessary, wouldn't it? They can replicate, in a manner of speaking. Anyway, you must have wondered who the next woman is going to be, the fifth?'

Beamish grinned, egging him to conclude the worse, then said, 'Easter is coming, will Mae get fat?'

'Leave her out of this, you bastard! If anything happens to her, I swear to you, I'll kill you!'

Smiley stood up, 'Sod your threats, Tinkerbell. You just get on and finish the dresses, the little special effects, the women are so finicky, you know.'

Sam could do no other than he was bid, but he knew he was getting nearer and nearer to cracking point.

CHAPTER TWENTY-FIVE

Sam was fighting hard to keep awake. His fingers were bloody and raw from the sewing and the cutting. They'd kept at him, especially that fucking Susannah, to finish their clothes, demanding the most finicky of alterations, often he knew to no purpose but vanity, one of them vying with the other in criticism, where no criticism was valid, just to appear to be more sophisticated.

The only bright thing in this dark nightmare was that he could from time to time believe that they hadn't got Mae. But if they had?

Sam looked up from his work, rubbed his eyes. The needle he was using had suddenly begun to shimmer, then instead of the tinge of green from the fluorescent light, he saw the spectrum. He looked up at a chandelier, instead of the muted rainbow in the glass pieces, a blaze of fractured light seemed to hurtle into his eyes like a blast of coloured glass from a blunderbuss. *He hadn't taken his tranquillisers.* He was experiencing a mild migraine, heralding the onset of a schizophrenic episode. He hadn't taken the pills because he hoped to save all of them for the mannequins, if not them, then Beamish, a calculated risk, and the gamble looked as if it wasn't paying off. He knew he had only hours before becoming incapacitated - unless he took his medication.

Anger choked him, he could scarce see the needle for it, and then he snapped, the accumulated rage and frustration of years, he stood up, and began to slash the dresses hanging on the racks with his shears. He started with Susannah's red silk, but before he could do any damage, with sickening abruptness, the four mannequins jerked out of their beds. Gleamingly naked, they went straight for Sam.

Josie knocked him off his feet, sending him two body lengths across the floor. She'd hit his spine, just above his waist. He crashed to the floor, doubled up foetally. He saw the hatred in her eyes, blazing blue eyes, and a perfect face contorted, nostrils flared, lips tight against bared teeth. *Christ, she 's going to eat me.*

Josie looked at her son, now beside himself with terror, reduced to a cowering, yet still thrashing, victim, held down on the floor like a floundering fish by her foot on his back, face down. My poor son, she thought, but she was powerless against the rage and hate inside her, hate and rage directed at him.

Susannah bent down close to him, 'You horrible little toe-rag,' she hissed, her green eyes hard as emerald in ice. 'Think your little tantrum is going to spoil anything? Well, you gutter-slob, we have plans for you, and you'll bloody well have to repair the damage you've done to our dresses so we can look our best tonight. Meanwhile, you'll be our guest to the making of Mae.'

At that moment Beamish came out of the lift carrying Mae.

Oh my gawd! Oh my gawd! the phrase went over and over in his mind, as if his mind were a catherine wheel spitting the words out as painful sparks.

Mae was struggling but could do nothing against Smiley's strength, and when Susannah took her, she could do even less, as strong hands ripped her clothes from her, and Bella helped Susannah to give her a shower, then dried her hair, combing it until it shone.

Sam tried to call out to her, but all he could do was grunt, while Mae up to this point had not seen him, and the grunting she did not recognise, understandably since Josie was pressing down on his chest, then his back, and at one time nearly throttled him by kneeling on his neck.

As the nightmare unfolded before him, Sam wept in impotence. Now he could do nothing, and what were they going to do to Mae?

For her part, Mae was half hypnotised by the attentions of Susannah, Joan and Bella, such beautiful creatures, and so gentle with her when she didn't struggle. Since it was impossible to make any headway against their amazingly strong hands, she took the sensible course and became compliant. Still she hadn't seen Sam.

'See?' said Susannah to Mae, as she held up a red dress, 'Isn't it beautiful? My uncle Justin made this for me when I was a young girl. I wanted you to have it, and when your change comes, I'm sure our dressmaker will make sure it fits you as well as the dresses he has made us.'

Mae blinked. The dress was beautiful, as was Susannah, but she would never be able to wear the dress, she was only five two, and Susannah was at least five inches taller, apart from the fact that she, Mae, had D-sized bras. Then the word dressmaker hit her. 'You have Sam! You have Sam! Let me see him!'

'Stay calm, little one. Everything will be all right, you'll just make matters worse if you kick up a fuss. Now, do you promise to be good?' Mae nodded. 'Well, just you gander round, and you'll see your Sam, right as rain.'

Mae turned, and at that moment Josie removed her foot and let Sam go. Mae finding herself free, ran towards him as he bounded to her. They met in a flurry of love, of concern, and embraced, tears of joy mixed with tears of anxiety. At first they were lost in one another, and then both stared wild-eyed at the circle around them - Bella, Josie, Joan, Smiley, and Susannah.

'What a lovely pair, and no mistake!' Susannah screeched. 'If you can love her, Sam, you standoffish sod, you can love us. Or to put it plainer than a pike, you'll learn to love us just like her!'

And then Susannah tore Mae from him, and he was held fast by Josie, as the other women took Mae to a pallet, the empty pallet, the fifth one.

'Don't struggle, Mae, or Sam will get it,' Susannah warned, as she laid her on the pallet facing her, Mae stock still, petrified. Susannah lay down with Mae facing her, then

Bella came and lay behind her. The scream never came out of Mae because Susannah pressed Mae's mouth with her own, slid her tongue down Mae's throat. Meanwhile, Bella caressed her. Mae was choking, but she felt a sweet effulgence pass into her, it had a narcotic effect, she was falling, falling, and yes, she was asleep, like in a dream. She was terribly hot though, and wanted the coolness of a kiss. Yes, the coolness of a kiss. The sweetness passed into her spine, and then spread down and up. When it got to her coccyx the warmth spread out to her loins. When it got to her brain, if filled her brain. Blood red. She was blood red, with an echoing voice within her head: I AM THE LADY OF THE TOMBS. SOME CALL ME MORNING STAR. I AM DEATH IN LIFE.

And I am bloody well Mae Fields, thought Mae, with cockney spunk. 'I'm Mae!' she screamed. 'Let me go!'

Laughter, echoing laughter, the smell of stinking fish, the odours of the sanctuary of lust, the perfumes of an old priestess, broken apples and spent seeds, wine gone bad under dancing feet, a broken bleeding skull: YOU SHALL BECOME ONE OF US.

It was all red. She could only see red, feel the women. Susannah's tongue was still in her, deep, deep within her, pumping something into her, a kind of ferment, making her grow - five inches in five minutes.

Pain erupted like a boil in her head, and then turned into a carnivorous flower, eating her brain. She could hear slurping, slopping sounds, and a harsh creaking, she felt she would be torn in two. Then her breasts began to shrink. The pain was frothy now, popping and bubbling. Her heart stopped beating, she knew her bones were dissolving. She could no longer cry out, but Sam, beside himself, was still struggling, in Josie's arms, and then as with a piercing scream, Mae felt herself fall into a pit of blackness, Josie hit Sam in the head with her fist, saying, 'No more to see for the while, poppet.'

When Sam recovered consciousness he was lying on the floor on his back, but he felt no pain. He could breath without pangs, and the throbbing from his mistreatment had abated. Relieved, he got up without difficulty, and saw there was a red-haired mannequin in the fifth cubicle, wearing nothing, lying on the bed, looking up at the chandelier. At first he thought it was Susannah. Then the sickening truth hit him, impacting slowly at first, then with the tumult of an avalanche as he saw that Joan, Bella, Josie - and Susannah - were lying in there cubicles. He rushed to the fifth cubicle to find the mannequin sitting up, smiling at him.

'Hello, Sam, I'm Mae. Aren't I beautiful?'

CHAPTER TWENTY-SIX

Sam smoked a cigarette and looked across to the pallet where Mae lay on her back, looking up at the chandeliers as if mesmerised by the candles in them, just as the other four were doing. It was like being stuck in a waxworks, he thought, with these bloody abortions doing their thing all around him, beautiful death dolls, and in one of them his little Mae was trapped.

He'd already known they could move and act like women, but they could also just be... mannequins, lying there gazing at the bloody chandeliers. But there were women inside these abominations. They hadn't spared him anything, they'd let Mae "come out". It wasn't a pleasant experience, change of size and all that, but there she'd been, his little Mae, and just as he was going to kiss her, glad she was back, she turned into one of *them* again, little five two into five seven. Jesus!

Oh yes, they'd egged him on, telling him to make love to the mannequin calling herself Mae, but he'd balked, and they weren't too pleased about that, but now they were quiet enough, resting up no doubt for the party, the great event when they were going to do something to him, or make him do something.

Now Mae was one of them, trapped in a living death. He yearned for little Mae again, with her own personal odour, her physical blemishes (that little wart at the back of her knee, set in the dimple crease, it had never seemed more important to him than now).

He was in a fix, they were both in a fix, but there had to be a way of winning. They had their weaknesses, they liked a tipple, and he had his medications... the problem was, if he hurt them, he hurt Mae, and what of his mother, Josie, could he ever help her now?

Somehow he had to make a move. There was no way, and when there was no way out, you went IN.

It was booze and tranquillisers at the first opportunity.
And then? What then?

Sod it! He could only do the best he could. He had to start
somewhere.

Beamish had lent him one of his suits, with a red
cummerbund, and now he was dancing with Susannah who
wore her favourite dress he'd made, of red silk, which showed
her beautiful body to great advantage. Beamish was dancing
with Mae, while the other three were at the wine table
drinking Margaux.

Susannah held him close as they swayed rhythmically to
Dusty Springfield singing that one about having more than a
skipping rope to lend - they loved these golden oldies, this
one was Josie's favourite. Sam saw that Bella and Josie were
getting up to dance with each other (he knew they liked to
dance with each other more than with a man, these women,
but they were also strangely conservative in some of their
social habits). Joan was alone, sipping her wine.

Without warning, Susannah roughly disengaged herself
from him, and he noticed how her eyes were shining even
brighter than usual, while above them the chandeliers swayed
slightly, sending shimmering light throughout vestibule. It
was as if a breeze had come into the vault, but how? And
then he saw that all five women were standing now, while
Beamish himself was on his knees.

'Kneel!' Susannah ordered, and Sam did as he was told.

The five women came together and linked hands, but they
did not form a circle, instead, each of them was the apex of a
five pointed star, the inward V's being made by their arms.

Fascinated, Sam heard them sing in beautiful unison, Mae
being as solemnly ecstatic as the rest, but he could not
understand the words, foreign certainly, continental probably
not.

The chandeliers quivered, as dark light, Sam could think
of no better description, descended from them and centred on

the living star, where it began to glow, and with a crack as sharp as lightening the light turned into a shimmering fluorescent figure of a woman, tall like the other five, similar to them in feature, but so much more beautiful, so much more... goddess-like, with her black hair shining metallic blue, her aquiline features sculpted to perfection, green eyes of piercing brightness, and a mouth of heart stopping sweetness and sensuality.

The five women slowly descended to their knees, all of them gazing in adoration at the Priestess, who touched them each on the lips with her fingertips, as with a smile she turned again into a cone of light, which with a lightening crack, became the shadows of the vault.

Rapturous, the women began to dance, a strange dance, in column, while Smiley came up to him. 'Drink and be merry, old son,' he said. 'You've got no idea how long Susannah has waited for this day. About time too.'

'What does it mean for me and Mae?' asked Sam, wondering if what he had seen was the beginning after all of a hallucination. Was the whole bloody thing one damn mind show? No, the original mind show years ago had been real.

'I don't know the details, mate, Susannah knows that. But it's not hard to guess, is it? You'll have to set up another sanctuary, continue the work. After all, these days growth is all the rage, isn't it?' Beamish chortled, slapped him on the back, 'Think of it, you'll never need the National Health.'

Sam only half heard him, but the message was clear, and as he watched Mae dance, he was overcome with a longing for *his* Mae, wanted a life with her. He'd take his chances, sod Smiley and his mother Susannah, and what they had devoted themselves to.

Beamish drifted away toward his glass. The women had paired up to dance again to golden oldies, while Sam saw that Joan had settled down again, was by herself at table, sipping wine.

Sam felt the phials of tranquillisers in his left trouser pocket. *You are going to have a deep sleep, girl,* he thought, *put your head to rest in modern magic, here comes the Medicine Man.*

He looked over to Beamish. The guy had a self-satisfied smirk which infuriated him.

The trick was going to be to get him spiked at the same time. Spike the raddled lot in one go, why not? Get it all over with. *You can't do that, it might kill Mae, might kill Josie. Then you could kill yourself.* No, it would be OK. Just enough to keel them over. He could tell by the way they were moving, just off beat, that they were getting pissed. So was Beamish, now carrying a large tumbler of Scotch as he wandered about close to the two pairs of women dancing, looking them over, smacking his lips appreciatively. Then Joan got up and took him for a dance.

Now was the time.

Sam ambled over to the wine table and spiked Beamish's glass and his Scotch bottle, then their wine bottle, guessing he had added many times the recommended dosage (written on the phial of Largactile). He had his back to them anyway, just for a moment, that was all that he needed. Ostentatiously, he topped up their glasses. Then he lit a cigarette, sat down, and waited.

They all came to the table, along with Smiley, for another drink.

It was an uncanny but beautiful sight. Five tall and exquisite women wearing wonderful party dresses. Mae had one of red silk, that had been a rush job, he'd been given Susannah's, 'the one my uncle Justin made me,' and told to adapt it. So he had, and he had to admit it looked pretty damn good.

They all sat down and proceeded to chatter amongst themselves, leaving Smiley and him out of it, for they were discussing men, fashion, and men, but their remarks on men would give no male any sense of security.

Beamish lit his cheroot, had his glass in his hand and gulped the lot back in one go.

Thank God for that, thought Sam, stunned by his good fortune. 'Lousy Scotch you serve,' Sam laughed, 'can't you crack up another? I can't stand this, tastes like a mouse pissed in it.'

Beamish grunted, got up and went to the drinks stashed in racks along the wall. 'Haig?' he called out.

'Sure,' Sam agreed.

He cast a glance at the women, they were sipping away, clearly oblivious to the taste. All they cared about was getting pissed.

In twenty minutes at the most, I'll be the only one awake. Was his conversation so boring then? His attempt at levity thrilled him as much as putting on a pair of wet pyjama trousers on a windy night.

Joan keeled over first, her head dropping with a soft plonk onto the table. She grinned, then fell asleep. Beamish, alarmed, went round to her, took one step, and then with a baleful look at Sam, slowly sank to his knees, rose again, then tried to grab the table for support, missed, and crumpled up, moaning, cursing, rocking his head back and forth as he sat on the floor his legs spread before him. Soon, he lurched back, striking his head sickeningly on the flagstones.

As all this happened the four other women looked dumbfounded.

Sam knew now it was a race between the drugs and their sense of danger.

Only Susannah appeared now to sense something amiss. She got up and advanced on him but he, anticipating her, also got up, resolving to keep out of her way.

'You bastard,' she screeched, 'what have you done?'

He bluffed it out, but kept moving away from her, 'Me? I've done nothing. Everyone just had too much to drink that's all.'

Susannah stopped, glass still in her hand, then slowly she fell to her knees, then keeled over.

Beamish snored great snorts as Sam took each comatose mannequin to their cubicle, then he rushed over to his work table, selected swathes of silk, one of the strongest of fabrics, cut wide ribbons, then rushed back to Beamish. Cackling inanely with terror, but triumphant, hardly able to co-ordinate his excited movements, he tied Smiley's hands, and his feet, and gagged him.

Overhead, the chandeliers tinkled, as if a sudden breeze disturbed them. The malevolence was palpable.

Susannah was flicking her eyelashes. He could see the agitation in her movements. She was pursing her lips, clenching her fists, *willing* herself into action against the drug.

He had to move fast.

CHAPTER TWENTY-SEVEN

Sam's fingers itched to hold a cigarette. There was a packet of Senior Service in his jacket. He retrieved it, got to the wine table, drank from the bottle. YOU JUST DRANK FROM THE SPIKED DRINK, YOU'LL BE OUT FOR THE COUNT LIKE THE REST IN HERE. Got hold of himself - saw it wasn't *that* bottle. Knowing though it could happen, he was so wound up, he smashed the wine bottle against the wall and then poured the remains of Beamish's drink on the floor. Got himself another bottle.

At his feet Beamish was still lying motionless. He looked down to check him over. *You'll have to kill him, you know that, kill him - can't do it in cold blood.*

He had to get them o-deed. Overdose. OD. But wait a moment, they are so physically weak, it might be possible to...

He went back over to where he'd smashed the bottle, picked up a sliver of glass, returned to Susannah. Nicked her arm. She whimpered. A clean wound parted like a mute mouth trying to speak. A bluish thick liquid seeped out from the pink lips.

Why not cut them up? Into little pieces? Yes, and that way have to cut up Mae and Josie. Besides, they might grow into new replicas, *each piece*. Like worms.

If only he could escape, get help.

Numbed, he realised that he had forgotten he could *leave* Convent. He trembled at that, and its implications: you could be got at so deeply that you no longer realised your own potentials and possibilities. His heart went out to all hostages. They might be sitting in front of an unlocked door, but terror had wiped out the possibility in their minds that the door could be opened.

Now the problem was time, they might come round any minute. He picked up the bottle of spiked Scotch. Now, which bitch to stuff the bottle in first and make her drink?

In his concern Sam forgot all about Beamish.

Susannah sat up.

Oh Christ!

With shaking hands he poured half the Haig, with its crushed phials of heavy, major tranquillisers down her spluttering throat.

'You toe-rag!' Susannah blubbered, choking on the dirty brown liquid, *but it was going down.*

She was rolling her eyes, and hissing at him with venomous hatred, but she had no more strength than an irritated kitten. The malevolence within her distorted her features, and her smell was that of the mortuary, without the disinfectant, a low searing stench that constricted his throat and belly, causing him to throw up violently.

She wriggled, almost got away, he pushed the bottle deeper into her throat as her struggles weakened.

Hoping that was enough, he stood back, his face white (where it wasn't bloody) with exhaustion. As he did so, Susannah found the strength to speak. Her voice was low, tense with effort, 'You are my grandson, how can you do such a thing?'

He looked up at the fading eyes, 'You know why, Susannah, you know why. My granny died a long time ago, and you were glad.'

He smelled jasmine and lilies, musk and frankincense, smells reeved together, like many griefs in a single sadness, coming from Susannah. Then a sour stench billowed from Susannah's decaying body. Soon she would be no more than a few dried pieces of bone and skin, her magnificent hair white, her wonderful eyes gone out for ever.

He stood aside, for there was fluid dripping from her.

Then her shoulders sagged, her neck broke, and plopping down at his feet was a putrescence liquid, on the bed a pile of meaningless skin and bones, topped by a skull, one with whisps of scanty hair, eye sockets of delicate fissured bone, and toothless jaws.

Now he knew what would happen.

He started on Joan. Then moved on to Bella. Then he lit a Senior Service with a Swan Vesta, slugged a Jack Daniels back, and watched.

Joan would rot like Susannah, she was so old. Bella though - she would be sixty. If she survived, then Josie would - and Mae would. But what if they didn't?

...he didn't know.

Joan's smell now was that of decay, the dead. Sewers on summer afternoons in London, leaking tunnels, which should have long been overhauled, but weren't. A smell of meat left in its plastic clingfilm, left for a fortnight, forgotten, and when you opened the door, the odour, the stench caressed your face before going into your nose and tangling with your brain - the clingfilm obscenely bulging and splitting like a fig, lips of meat squirming through the split. Wet meat smell. Or beans left to rot in the sun, after a boil up, red kidney beans, forgotten about. The death when you pithed an animal, cut off steaks. But there was another death, the death when meat putrefied. She had both deaths in her.

Sam watched Joan in horror. She was deflating. The fullness of her thighs were turning into thin shanks upon which yellowing blotched skin wrinkled. She coughed, and spat out a swatch of teeth, embedded in thick green phlegm.

Oh, God, this will happen to Mae, to Josie. No. No. Hold on to yourself. Think it through. Joan was at least a hundred and thirty years old, give or take a few years. Freed from pickling (he could not think of any other terms) effect of being in a replica (which he'd killed), of course she must attune to her real age.

She was coughing and wracking, vomiting gouts of red-black blood, her body now sticklike, the beautiful dress lying almost flat against her thigh bones. Her knees looked enormous. Then the death rattle, her eyes imploring, her tongue trying to speak, but unable to form words. Her eyes broke and fell into their sockets, blueish and virulent. The smell was gangrenous. Now the corpse will decay. The corpse will decay. Liquidly. Squirmingly. And then it was over.

Joan now was just skin and bone. Dried. Mummified.

'Sam.' The voice was low, and weak. It was Bella. He whirled round. An old woman of sixty sat on the bed. Her beautiful silk dress seemed incongruous on her, but her figure was still good, just a little sagging of breasts, which were too large for the blue chiffon and cotton creation, and a slackness of the thighs. She still had one court shoe on, but her stockings were laddered and reeved. Her blonde hair was white, her face though attractive, bore the unmistakable signs of grief and age, but her eyes flickered with life.

'Is it you, Bella, is it you?' he asked hoarsely.

'Yes, Sam, it's me, cock.'

He looked across to Mae. She was still a mannequin, as was Josie. Happiness thrilled through him, all he had to do now was free them both.

Carefully, Sam poured the spiked drink into Josie's mouth, and then into Mae's. Shaking with expectation, he held Mae's hand, waiting for her to come through. Willing her to live.

Suddenly, Sam felt a hand grab him by the throat. The hands were strong, he was choking, he feverishly, desperately pawed at the fingers around his throat, and tried to bend them back, heard one snap, and then he was unconscious, as with hate and malice, Beamish took Sam down to the pit, and threw him in it.

CHAPTER TWENTY-EIGHT

When Bella awoke, she felt tired and worried, but did not know why she was worried. She turned, and saw Josie except that she did not know it was Josie - Josie had black hair, was a young woman, this person was a stranger, an old woman with white hair. Where was Josie? When she passed her dressing mirror she saw a strange old lady in it. It couldn't be *her*, because she had blonde hair, big breasts and an unlined face. The woman peering anxiously back at her had fallen breasts, white hair, and a very lined face. In astonishment at what she was seeing, she brought her hand to her mouth, and the woman in the mirror did the same thing.

Oh my gawd!' she screamed, 'oh my gawd!'

Her scream had frightened Josie, who saw an old woman screaming, 'Help me!' She went over. Who was this woman? She wanted to help. Within moments, there were two old women looking into the mirror screaming...

When Mae came round and saw the messes that had once been Susannah and Joan, and then saw two old ladies, she blocked her ears against their screaming and to hold in her own panic; then to her amazement she saw the two of them start drinking at a table, as if there was no tomorrow. Trying to escape, Mae thought.

She got off the pallet.

No help from them. Where was Sam? Where was Smiley?

CHAPTER TWENTY-NINE

At the bottom of the pit, Sam knew all things and nothing. He was everywhere, and nowhere. He was all powerful and had no power. He knew the secrets of the future and the errors of the past, but he was in NOW and could not tell he was.

But this was how it had always been, for twenty years he had known this hell of nothingness and everything. (Flowing water, water full of waste, water where brown and pink rats lived, swam and snickered, pink tails acting as rudders in the black eddying water, hear the sound of water trickling over sluice gates, and the echoing of the Thunder God in the far distance.) BWHAM. BWHAM. BWHAM. BWHAM. NOTHING UNUSUAL ABOUT THUNDER GODS, KNOWN THEM FOR TWENTY YEARS. IN THIS HOSPITAL AND THAT, IN THIS PADDED CELL AND THAT, AFTER A WHILE THE WORLD OF THUNDER GODS IS A PLACE YOU CAN LIVE IN. THE OLD DOCTORS USED TO HAVE THE IDEA THAT WHAT WOULD SEND A SANE PERSON MAD MIGHT SHOCK AN INSANE PERSON BACK TO SANITY, SO THEY INVENTED THE SNAKE PIT AND PUT THE SLOBBERING PARANOIC INTO IT. WOKE UP TO FIND HIMSELF SURROUNDED BY SNAKES (AND DID NOT TAKE ANY NOTICE).

Sam woke up to find himself in the Pit. He looked up and saw a rectangle of light above him. How far up? About a hundred feet. He looked around him and could see very little, except the rats as they scudded across the black slick of water which went through the centre. He was lying on a soft pile of... just like the rubber room. You woke up in a rubber room and the light of the bulb filled everything, especially your own head. There was yellow rubber on the floor and on the four walls. No windows, and you could barely find out where the door was. No handle. Nothing but rubber, six faces of rubber, even the ceiling, six faces of your cube of incarceration. No window, no door, no furniture - just the sick sweet smell of vomit, of shit, of piss, of sweat, and of fear, as you lay there wondering what they had put on you - the linen of the straitjacket cut into your muscles, and you could not breathe too well. Lucky sometimes if they shot you full of a tranquilliser, otherwise you went through hell... So waking up in a pit with a light a hundred feet above, and rats swimming in flowing black water was not much to get hung up about. (*Your mind would produce worse any second now, you did not have your medication...*) The Thunder God would Thunder. (His heart.) Sam tried to get up from the mixture of clay, loam, refuse, and lime, but found himself digging deeper into it. He came across a wizened corpse, its teeth grinning at him, shockingly white teeth which reflected light from the spotlight blazing into the Pit from above, from the lower chamber.

Old son, been here long? You should meet some of the buddies I have buried in my brain, who will resurrect unless I get my medication... please God, my medication, the shots of life which will still the demons of my brain (not a bad place this, stinks a bit, but the rats just stand on their back feet and look at me, pink eyes baleful, teeth dirty yellow, and those naked tails, yuk, not a pretty sight) BEEN IN WORSE PLACES THAN THIS, SAM. YOU HAVE IT MADE HERE (just give me my pills and I can cut it anywhere - would like a smoke, hungry too) he tried again to get up.

Got a problem somewhere, cannot get up (he did not know it, but his thigh muscles were badly torn; they were still functional, but any real extension there would cause the pain of the rack). AAAAAAWWWCGGHHHH! His scream echoed in the Pit. Trouble somewhere. He shook his head, trying to clear it. Mild concussion.

How the hell can you fall a hundred feet and live? You fall on this soft compost of bodies and lime, but mainly, when they tossed you in, you hit the side, which sloped down to this flooring, which was only about seven by seven, sloped all the way, and see your fingers - his nails were torn out, he had no nails on the first three fingers of each hand, torn out, scraping into the side, holding on. His chest was in tatters, and so were his loins and thighs, (at one time you were upside down, still you held on) so you just hit here and lived. (Maybe like a a baby, see the story regular as clockwork in the papers, BABY THROWN OUT OF WINDOW LIVES. BABY IN CAR ACCIDENT. PARENTS DEAD. BABY LIVES. Something about relaxation, and after you have been shafted the way the mannequins could, shamefully, he was just pure relaxation (blood tricked between his buttocks). Try to get up again, old son.

This time Sam got up, stifling the scream from the pain in his leg. Once up, he didn't care about the pain. There was too much going on in his head to bother about physical pain. Had to hold on.

Why?

What was the purpose? You have a purpose. In the rubber rooms, only purpose is to endure. But *now* you have a purpose. (What is the purpose?) He didn't know why he was here.

...sudden image of Mae... Purpose. He had a purpose.

They wouldn't put you down here if there was a way out. That is why they put you in the rubber room, because there was no way out, and they could forget all about you, outside you were too much of a problem. In there (here) you are no problem any more. But there was always a way out when you still lived. Trick with the straitjacket was easy - you tensed all your muscles as they put it on, that gave you a purchase when they left you had a few centimetres of movement, and you could do it. He did it once, just the once, got out of it, but he learned never to do that again, because the next time they put two on him, and they dampened the outer one with water, so he almost choked to death when it shrank on him. Always a way out though.

Sam looked around him, his eyes wild and glittering in the harsh spotlight. The floor of the pit was a midden, the water just about got through the refuse, but he could see that sometimes the level had risen several feet, during floods he guessed - above his head, you could see the striations in the wall, different colours. It wasn't uniform, centuries of use of this land, ever building up, had left foundation after foundation. Arch. There was an arch. Just how deep is the water? Arch. There is a grey limestone arch, at one end of the rivulet, follow the rivulet, another arch. Just how deep is the water?

Sam bent down on the decomposing rubbish which formed the bank he was on, and dipped his arm into the stream. It was horribly cold, and the rats were closer now, looking at him with baleful stupid eyes. It was deeper than arm's length. What if you got in and swam under the arch? Would you drown? Maybe it led to a sewer network, this was sewer water. Condoms, lavatory paper floated by, human turds floated. Maybe...

Shock of cold water streaking past, in your hair, your eyes, your ears. Cold, yet no different from laying in an isolation room, naked on the floor, waking at night (day?) and seeing nothing but blackness, shaking with cold, no window, and the door has no handle, no rectangle of light, all you do is hold your breath to keep in the scream. But here, here you can swim too...

Sam was in a bricked conduit, barely four feet in diameter. It was full, with only an inch or so gap between the top of the arch and the stream flow. The current was strong enough to push him along, but he was wriggling too, his arms outstretched in front of him, one leg paddling behind. He turned over from time to time, gulping water and air into his lungs, scraping his nose on the limed surface of the conduit.

When you are suffocating in a shrinking straitjacket you have a choice of madnesses: you can have the madness of knowing what is happening to you, and the alternative of screaming so you go into a black pit of terror. It is not much of a choice. His screams echoed along the foaming filthy surface of the stream, but he felt the straitjacket of the water and it was freer than usual, so his scream was not so important. He chose the madness of knowing... In a floating isolation room they have put out the light and your sweat is between you and the chafing of the straitjacket. You survived that many times, the isolation room, you survived the drugs and the room and the jacket you just do what can be done. His hands stretched out further, he paddled hard with his legs-

-and just as he was going to suck in the last lungful of water he was precipitated ten feet down into a main sewer conduit, fully ten feet in diameter, and only half full. Here the current was very strong, and he lay on his back in the pitch blackness, breathing well, with the occasional racking coughing fit, as he spewed up water and detritus.

Sam breathed in the clean air, and squelched along as water ran off his soaking clothes, his feet spreading out on the hard paving stones.

He'd come up in a derelict street to the South of Convent, one where the houses were being demolished for new tower blocks, recognised where he was, and made his way towards Christ Church steeple. It was still dark, cold enough for his breath to form clouds as he breathed out, hurting his lungs as he breathed in.

He was near to breaking point, the orange lights would suddenly shatter into a wildly spinning spectrum of all the colours, which themselves would mate and change, full of hissing inner white light, sharp as broken glass at the edges.

Soon (how soon?) he knew that there would be sounds as well, at first just roaring and shouting with no discernible pattern, voices snatched out of streets and amplified, streets of long ago, of voices the owners of which had long forgotten what they said. Then there would be chaos in his thinking, he would be at the mercy of the first network which fired off in his head. There was no way of telling what it would be, could be the rape, the beating, could be a memory of something wonderful, like Mae, but he would not be able to control it, its direction, or even duration, and then over that would come the hallucinations of sight and sound. After that assault there would be paranoia, he would see, actually see inside his head, one of those women tearing him apart, slopping bits of his body against walls, dragging pulped legs, his pulped legs around, as he threshed armless and legless on the cobbles - he was now in Spitalfields.

You can't go to Convent. You can't go. You will be killed this time. Ring Dr Harowitz, get medicated, then you can really help. No time. I know there is no time.

He stood stock still as the porters bustled about him, as fruit was unloaded from lorries which had started in Holland, France, Germany, as vegetables from the world over were trundled past him on trollies that had been used for more than half a century, their iron shod wheels clattering harshly over the cobbles. 'Watch yorself, cock!' He didn't fully know what they meant, as they shouted 'Watch your back!', and other kindly meant warnings as the men went about their work.

Mae needs me, I've got to get back.

Sam saw the light go out over Convent's front door. He had never seen it out at night before, used to look at the white sphere from his studio, was on from dusk to dawn. (But the brain light was going faster, and breaking up, like an exploding miniature galaxy.)

Convent's light had gone out. (Lights exploding in his brain.) Then a flash of realisation: something is going on, NOW, in Convent. Got to get there.

GOT TO.

He braced himself against the pain of his leg, and was about to run, when a police car stopped on the cobbles in front of him. Two officers got out, waylaid him.

'You all right, *sir*?' asked the shorter cop, peering up into Sam's face.

CHAPTER THIRTY

After throwing Sam into the pit, Smiley, as a precautionary measure, had turned off the electricity supply to Convent, thereby immobilising the lifts. Consequently he had to go down the spiral staircase to Vestibule, but Mae heard him - 'Is that you, Sam?' - no answer, so just as he was about to insert the key into the locked door, she rammed Sam's shears into the keyhole.

'That won't do you any good, you slag!' Smiley bellowed, and she heard him going back up the steps, no doubt to get some tool for opening the door, but she hadn't heard him take the key out.

Shaking with fright, Mae was trying to control herself. She saw Bella and Josie were getting drunker, looking at her, confused, angry and hating - how would you like to be beautiful for decades? they seemed to be saying, and suddenly be turned into an old hag?

Oh, malakry! this was all she needed - she had to get out. She banged the door, twiddled with the shears, but the key was partially turned, and would not fall out.

She went over to the drinks rack and brought two bottles of whisky and one of vodka, then she got all the material he could from Sam's worktable, piled it by the door, smashed the bottle tops, poured their contents over the clothes and wood, then she lit the bonfire with a match. A blueish flame leapt up against the oaken planks, seemed to recoil, and then took hold of the cloth, turning from blue to yellow. There was very little smoke, at first, but was soon copious, and was dragged by draught up the spiral staircase, filling the passageway with choking smoke, some of it coming from burning nylon and other manmade fibres, thick black smoke.

'Any identification?' It was the shorter cop talking.

Sam shook his head, 'I'm Sam Reese, that's my studio over there.' He nodded towards his shop. 'I want to get back and have a shower, change my clothes.'

He toyed with the idea of asking for their help, but there was no time. If he did persuade them to come over to Convent, they wouldn't let him get in and do what he wanted to, had to, there would be interminable talking on their portable radios. Besides, what could he say? (Soon you won't be able to say anything.) Besides, did he really want *anyone* to hear about this?

The taller cop spoke to his colleague, 'He smells like a latrine.'

(Don't run. Brazen it out. No time. Must run.) He forced himself to speak carefully, though the scream of frustration was building up in him. (Mind-lights. Kaleidoscope. Shattering mirrors. Cut your brain to pieces soon.) 'I'm on my way home, I don't need any help.'

They could see he was not drunk, it was just that he was wet, and looked lost. No shoes. But no law against that. Maybe high on something. No sign in the pupils - the shorter one was shining a torch into Sam's face, gazing at him intently. The taller one said, 'Come on, let's leave him to it.'

(Thank God!)

'Naw, hold on a minute,' said the shorter one.

Through the crackle of the flames, Mae heard Smiley coming down again, heard him cough, then suddenly the door shook and a mighty echoing crashing splintering sound went round Vestibule. Sledgehammer or axe, or pick-axe.

She had some respite when Smiley had such a violent coughing fit, he had to go back up. He returned with a fire extinguisher, squirted it through the keyhole, the cracks at the side and the gap at the bottom. The foam crept like a giant amoeba, killing the fire, then the thundering, splintering crashes began again.

Smoke did indeed ascend but by the time it reached the top of the second set of steps it was so attenuated, it would not be noticeable from the street.

Mae began piling furniture against the door, but there was no one thing heavy enough to prevent the door being forced. She couldn't move Sam's worktable because it was screwed into the flagstones by rawplugs at the bottom of its feet. Probably too heavy, anyway.

Too late, Mae suddenly realised what the cessation of sound implied. She heard the slide of a key, and saw it its haft come through, turn, but She couldn't get to it because of the piled furniture - the shears had long since fallen out through vibration.

The door inched steadily against the furniture, with Mae pushing back, but it was an unequal struggle, for Mae, for all her tearing her lips with her teeth in determination, could not decide the issue with her 110 pounds. And there was no help possible from Bella and Josie, who still in shock, were trying to get plastered and blot out the knowledge of what they had suddenly become.

(*'Why are you wet? Catch your death of cold,'* said the runt. *'No law against being wet.'*) **I GOT TO GO**.

Smiley crashed the door open.

Shaking, grim faced, Mae went for him with a broken bottle, one she'd used to start the fire. Mae got one jab in, slicing the bottle across Smiley's mouth, the sharp edges of glass ripped his lips and nose up in pink gashes, which then gouted blood. He backhanded her, sending her sprawling.

(*Sam said, 'Can I go now?' 'Just hold on a minute, sir.'*)

Methodically, Smiley locked the door, retrieved Sam's shears, dragged Mae over to the altar, and slung her on it, tying her with red silk ropes, by wrist, and ankle, wracking her out.

Smiley stared down at her. 'Going to sacrifice you, cut you up, slow, real slow. But first I'm going to rape you, get it? What they did to Our Lady, what was done to her, I'll do to you. You for her.'

Mae screamed terror and defiance, 'Curse you both! Curse you all!'

Smiley merely smiled, coldly, the knowledge in his eyes that this woman was his, and he saw she knew that too, but she could not know how fearful he was that it might not work, that Eskalith would die. More blood. More living blood.

CHAPTER THIRTY-ONE

Sam looked down at the shorter cop, who seemed to dislike having to look up so far. Sam wondered where they were getting them these days, this guy could not have been more than five- seven, so he towered over him by eight inches. The taller cop, about his height, clearly wanted to go. What was there for him in spending time on yet another eccentric? But he had to follow along with his colleague for a while.

'Is it normal to be wet and stinking like you are, son?' the short cop asked, all pretence of civility gone.

Sam had a hunch this little shit would never let go, keep on at him until he found something to drag him in for. That realisation, with almost the last of his will power, spurred him to make a stab at turning the guy aside. 'I'm not indecently dressed. I don't have to explain to you why I'm in this state. So why are you harassing me?'

'You *look* suspicious,' runty replied.

Then the car radio whined their call sign, Sam heard the controller say they were needed, urgently. Fracas in Aldgate. The tall cop said, 'Get in, we can't 'ang about with him, not now.'

With sneering reluctance the short cop joined his partner, and with a bleating wail, the car thrashed out of Spitalfields.

Sam was running before they left, to Convent.

Josie and Bella were entirely unprepared for what happened next, at the hands of a man they had come to trust.

Smiley came up to them at the table, and with an arcing sweep of the shears took their throats out in one. Even as they spurted their life blood out upon the floor, and were falling, he was upon Bella, working with a will, slashing, gouging, ripping.

161

Sam climbed over the graveyard wall to Convent, ran up to the kitchen door, which he found open. He tried a switch, but all he got was a dull click, no answering light. (Why would anyone turn the power off?) He tried another switch, same result (Why had someone turned the power off?) The lights in his head were more glaring and vibratory by the minute.

He could smell smoke, and followed it to its source, finding himself at the door to Crypt, tried it, but it was locked. The only way down was by lift, unless he forced the door. What would he force a door with? (Trying hard to keep coherent lines of thought, but you haven't got much time. No plan either. You came here with good intentions but no plan.)

Smiley looked up from his work on Bella at the chandeliers as they trembled as if a breeze, a gentle, growing breeze was passing through them. His expression softened, there was hope now. Yes, he'd done enough. Time for the ritual rape, the mutilation. He went over to Mae, shears in hand, loosening his clothing.

- There was sufficient light from street lamps for Sam to find his way around, and he got to the cupboard under the stairs which he thought would house fuse boxes. Inside, he felt along the row of switches, and found one down. He pushed it up. Electric light flared on in the hall.

Sam was coming to the cusp of his sanity, and would soon move into the world he knew so well but could not control, but at this cusp, he was physically unrestrainable. They used to put him in straitjacket so he would not harm anyone or himself, and get him sedated, in that or reverse order - anything to calm the human cyclone that he was. He did have a plan, he knew he could take out Smiley when he was in this condition. It had taken more than five strong men to restrain him when he raged. (Tear the swine apart) (That's not a plan, what about the women? Don't know. Anything, but get Mae out.

The lift!

He got to it and pressed the button. The lift came up. The access doors hissed open. No one in there. Now what? He got in. Then the lift descended.

Smiley heard the lift, left Mae, and went over to the doors, waiting, shears ready.

The doors opened.

But nothing came out, because Sam stayed in, right against the wall, knowing that someone was waiting for him. The figure in front of him was Beamish. In a split second he took in that there was not a mannequin in sight, but he could see corpses it seemed strewn everywhere - but there was something, someone? writhing on the altar. Where was Mae?

Beamish came straight at him, his face purple with rage, his clothes covered in congealing blood.

The shears came straight at Sam's bowels, but he side-stepped, the tips of the blades ripping his shirt. Keeping his momentum Sam rushed past Smiley out into Vestibule, while Smiley, in his headlong rush crashed into the steel wall at the back of the lift.

Sam 's head was filled with broken lights. Oh God! Then he heard Mae - it was her voice, yes, yes! - scream, 'Press the lift button!'

Sam hesitated, Smiley was turning, to attack again. The button! Sam reached out, and found it, and pressed - the doors began to close, but Smiley got an arm through, and the doors began to open, so Sam pressed the button again, and kept it pressed. He was just able to reach the hand that held the shears while still pressing the button, thanks to his height. One of those fingers is broken, looks broken. He began to break the other fingers, bending them back until they snapped, one at a time, by the third, he had hold of the shears. Sam slashed at the wrist. Blood gouted out of the severed artery. Then the other hand came through. Just how long before he falls from loss of blood? Sam hacked at the other flailing hand. He got to the bone, and sawed. Just how long can he last loosing so much blood? (Haven't got much time. Light breaking into pieces, red, blue, yellow pieces. Air turning into metal. Not much time) *Hand. Kill hand.*

'Go for it, Sam!' Mae yelled, her voice breaking with hope and fear.

Sam hacked at it. Smiley cursed and wailed. Sam kept hacking, then sliced into the artery. A second gout of blood, spurted. He kept hacking, and then first one hand, and then the other, withdrew, and the doors closed.

He must have near bled to death. It's OK.

Steel doors, blood on steel doors. Who? Who is that person in the reflection of the steel door? You. You?

'Sam!'

Voice... where voice? Steel door shimmering, like that of a furnace, glowing white.

'Sam!'

Must kill the furnace.

'Sam!'

Mae could see Sam had little left. She saw him staring at the lift doors. Mesmerised. She kept shouting, but it was only when she screamed, 'Help me, Sam!' that he turned away from the doors, eyes glazed, and came towards her, shears in hand.

A woman. A red-haired mannequin woman. *Wearing a red dress..* Kill her, kill the mannequin woman.

Mae, sensing his confusion, shouted, 'It's me! Mae! The little one. Too short! TOO SHORT!'

Sam stopped, looked... *too short*, just a girl. MAE.

Yes... but...

Just one pill, one little 10 mg pill of Haloperidol would quiet the storm in his head, cohere light again, let him think.

'On the table, Sam, in the bottles!'

Sam bounded over to the bottle and took a swig, then bounded back to the altar to Mae and cut her bonds. They kissed, but not for long.

Sam, his head clearing rapidly, knew he had to make sure about Smiley. He went to the lift and pressed the button, watched as the near handless man came into view. Smiley glared at him with hate and reproach, but he was fading fast, time catching him up at last. He reverted to his true age, so that all that was left in his suit was a mummified skeletal figure, brown wrinkled skin on weak bones. Curiously, his teeth were still good, giving a fearsome grimace to the eyeless fleshless, hairless, scabbed, skull.

Then most poignant of all, there came from the corpse the smell of fresh roses.

He turned back to Mae, who was trembling, he hugged her, though scanning the place, all seemed quiet.

Was Mae going to flip? Was he? 'Have a stiff drink,' he said. They both had Scotch. He looked at her to see if she was thinking the same thing. She was, she looked around the shambles too. If the cops came here... Christ! Sam grabbed another Scotch bottle, drank deep. They sat at a table, and drank silently for some minutes. Sam wanted a cigarette, there was a packet on the table. He took one and gave one to Mae. It was good, good, in the lungs. There was no way this shambles could every be explained. Endless days in court, branded homicidal maniacs (Broadmoor here we come), or murderers (life imprisonment): lives ruined.

(Faint rustle of chandelier crystal, candles paling, darker shade of pale, sour smell now, deepening to a foetid cloud.

'Let's go, Mae. I've had enough.'

'We can't just go, you know that...' Mae trailed off, she was getting the picture: NEVER LIVE GOOD AGAIN IF THIS GETS OUT. *Susannah.* That corpse was no more than a mummy - a hank of hair, brown skin, and bones. If Forensic could determine age, it would be found to be one hundred and eighteen years. Couldn't be murder. (Who lives to one hundred and eighteen?) Same thing with *Joan*. (Dump them in the Pit.) But *Josie* and *Bella*? (Don't think about his mother, DON'T.) Freshly mutilated corpses of women in their sixties. That was the rub.

Beamish's corpse, good as one hundred. But people knew him. Would his disappearance be noted? Why not put a notice on the door announcing cessation of business? It all came down to the same thing, *nobody must see what was here*.

And there was more. She knew things Sam could never know - she had once been one of them.

Out of the corner of her eye she saw something move. She turned, and cried out. Josie was sucking up Bella's and Joan's blood, changing back into the lovely form she had inhabited for so many years, and then she changed into an even more beautiful woman, one with honeyed skin, an aquiline nose, a cupid bow mouth, a woman who looked with fierce yet beautiful green eyes.

Startled, Sam turned round to see what had gained Mae's attention. That fucking Josie was coming back! Was it never over? But he was up and at her in a split second, savagely snatching up a bottle of spiked drink. 'Right up *your* nose, this time!'

But Mae got there first.

Stupefied, Sam saw she was...

...*shielding* Josie, no not Josie, just wearing her clothes. 'Mae-!'

'No! Sam! NO! You mustn't destroy this body, it's Eskalith, transforming Josie. Don't you see? You can't kill Eskalith, but you can *trap her*.'

'What...?'

Sam looked intently at Mae, trying to divine her meaning.

The woman was trying to sit up, but couldn't make it.

'Don't you see? She won't be able to resist it. Eskalith has waited untold centuries to be beautiful again. She at last found Susannah, and the rest, now she has formed her own shape again. Once in, how could she tear herself away? Don't you *see*?

They were silent, the woman blinked.

Then Mae said, 'With dignity, Sam, I was one of them, with Eskalith, for a while. For all the hate, she remembers she was beautiful, so do it with dignity.'

EPILOGUE

"If you are reading this, it means I am dead, because you have my keys, and no one could hold them if I were still alive.

You are probably Sam, or Mae, no one else, unless Sam and Mae are dead too, because they wouldn't let anyone in Convent.

If they are dead, the rest is of no concern to you - but

Sam? (the peerless designer, who learned his trade at the feet of the dead, yet spurned the beauty that rose from the dead, the sentimentalist who would not learn to love, but preferred to disperse his brain in LSD, and then nursed hatred for all that gave him meaning).

Mae? (the stainless, the immaculate, who was given the gift of beauty, of immortality, and yet refused to collect her Temple Hire - receive it now, and remember you once were one of us).

- one, or both, this does concern you.

I give all my possessions to you, in equal portions. You will find schedules of what that entails. *The condition is that Convent be bricked up.*

And if strangers' eyes are reading this, then curse you.

Beamish Smiley"

Sam frowned, then chuckled, the old sod was game to the end, made him give a fuck. But you didn't have to worry about Eskalith, Beamish, you see, Mae understood. I know that bricking up Vestibule and Convent was for her peace, a little peace, but we've done much better than that. Can you see, Beamish, from your grave in the Pit, Josie, Joan and Susannah? I hope you can, you old sod, it'll be good for the cockles of your evil but loving heart.

Sam put the letter back in Smiley's safe, and locked it.

It was now a fine June in Charnegate, Convent was bricked up (he'd first read the letter and Smiley's instructions on getting back from Casualty at the London Hospital, neatly stitched up.

There had of course been another letter saying that he, Beamish, was in Argentina. Another document testified that Mae Fields, Sam Reese, either or both, had his power of attorney.

Sam was over in Convent now, checking everything was all right (it was) and to look at the schedule again - forty odd pages of hand-written items of wealth. Smiley had been fabulously wealthy - money from the women. Deposit Accounts. Properties scattered over London, some intended to be Sanctuaries.

In his old kitchen, Sam handled a phial of his medication between thumb and forefinger. 'You know,' he said wistfully, 'even if I hadn't taken LSD and told them what happened to me, told them about all this... reality, they would still have thought I was nuts.'

Mae kissed him, 'What will you tell Jacob?'

'I'll just ask him to start reducing the dosage,' he replied, then laughed, holding Mae tight. 'Paris, New York, here we come!'

Mae felt the hope in him, and it was good. So good. Would he ever remember they'd met before? If so, good; if not, he loved her now.

At Convent the lights were all out, the windows bricked up, and the doors all locked. There was a soft pool of moonlight over the eaves, you could hear the rustling of feathers as ring doves settled deeper into their plumage, raising the spines so they could trap more air, and so keep warm. In the graveyard yew trees, sparrows were silent, sitting on the branches, waiting for morning.

In Vestibule, illumined by candlelight, six tall candles in silver candelabra encircling her, Eskalith stood decked with jewels and wearing a scarlet dress, made by Sam, before a full length mirror. (*She is so beautiful. I am so beautiful.*) Her eyes glittered in the shifting yellow light, and her lips parted in a slow smile. *I am so beautiful.*

There were times when she actually thought the long hard exile from Babylon had come to an end - when she wasn't *just waiting.*

THE END